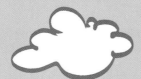

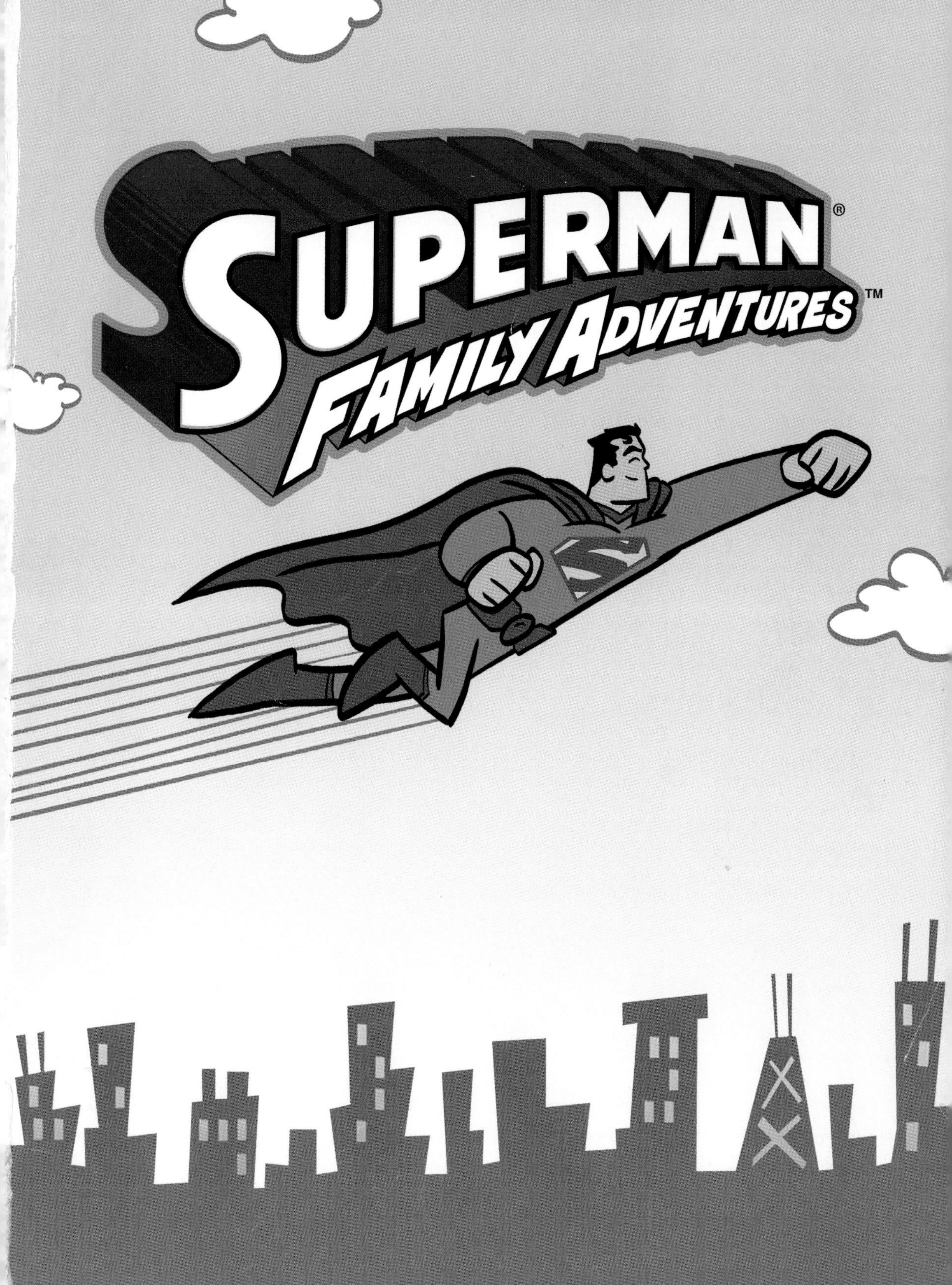
SUPERMAN®
FAMILY ADVENTURES™

STONE ARCH BOOKS
a capstone imprint

▼▼ STONE ARCH BOOKS™

Published in 2013
A Capstone Imprint
1710 Roe Crest Drive
North Mankato, MN 56003
www.capstonepub.com

Originally published by DC Comics in the U.S. in single
magazine form as SUPERMAN FAMILY ADVENTURES #5.
Copyright © 2013 DC Comics. All Rights Reserved.

DC Comics
1700 Broadway, New York, NY 10019
A Warner Bros. Entertainment Company

Cataloging-in-Publication Data is available at the
Library of Congress website:
ISBN: 978-1-4342-4793-3 (library binding)

Summary: Who is the mysterious Purple Superman? Is he trouble? Is
he a hero? Does Lois have a crush on him? Why does Superman feel
sick when he gets near him? And who's that new intern at the Daily
Planet?

STONE ARCH BOOKS
Ashley C. Andersen Zantop Publisher
Michael Dahl Editorial Director
Donald Lemke Editor
Brann Garvey Designer
Kathy McColley Production Specialist

DC COMICS
Kristy Quinn Original U.S. Editor

Printed in China by Nordica.
0413/CA21300442
032013 007226NORDF13

SUPERMAN® FAMILY ADVENTURES™

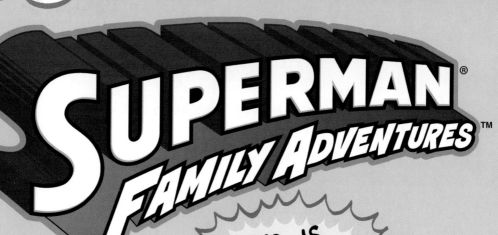

WHO IS THE PURPLE SUPERMAN?!

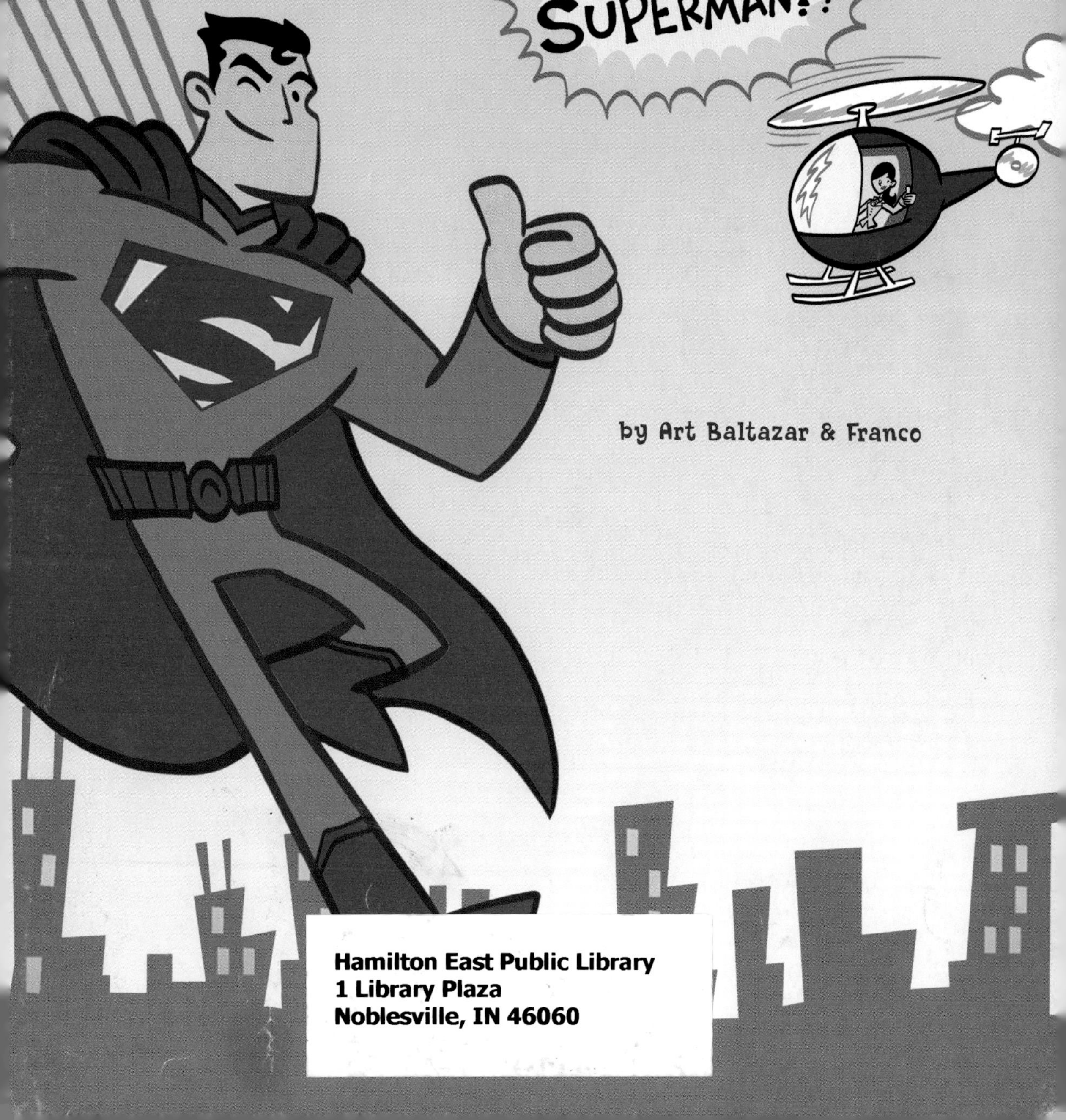

by Art Baltazar & Franco

SUPERMAN® FAMILY ADVENTURES™

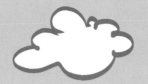

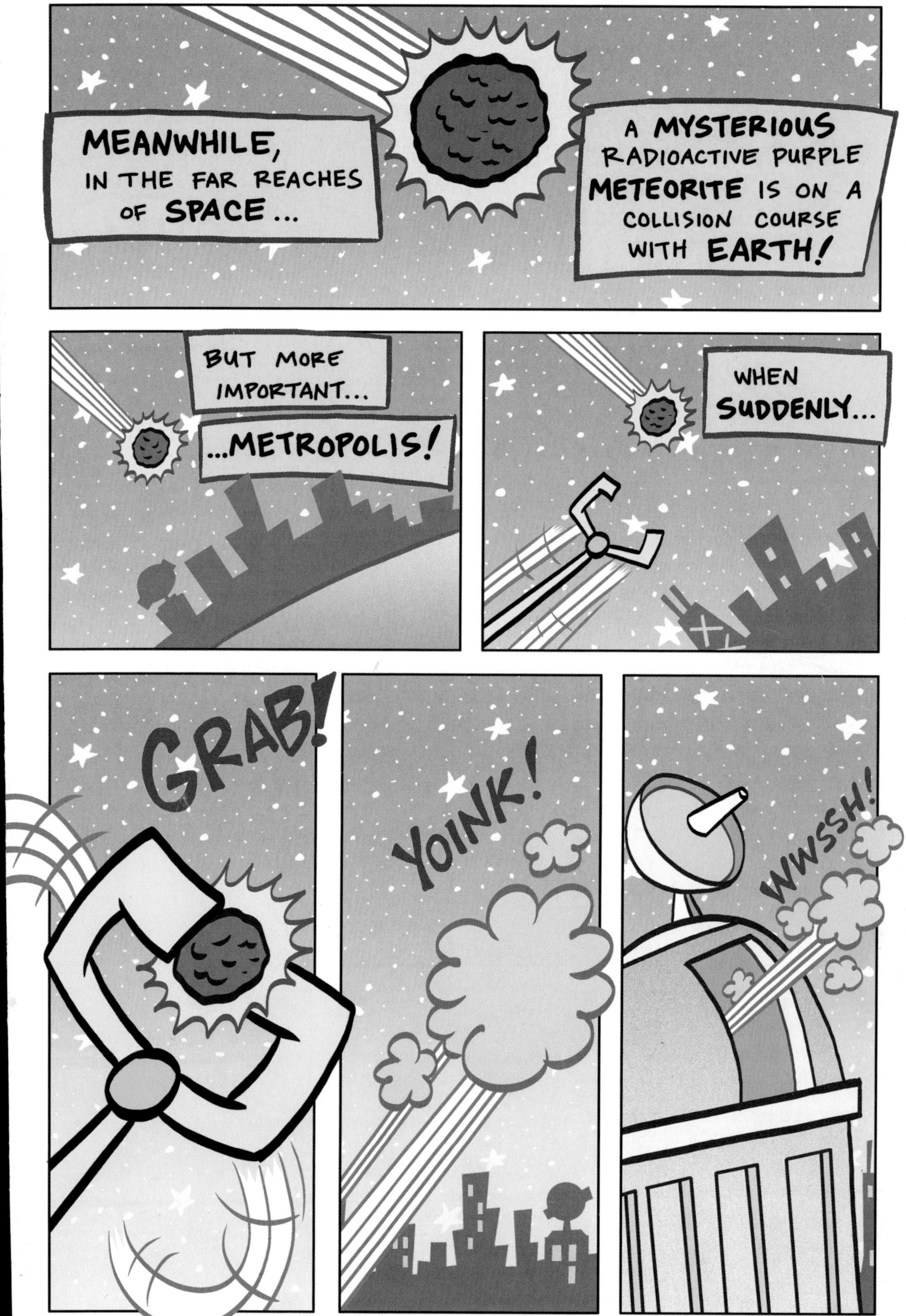
MEANWHILE, IN THE FAR REACHES OF SPACE...
A MYSTERIOUS RADIOACTIVE PURPLE METEORITE IS ON A COLLISION COURSE WITH EARTH!
BUT MORE IMPORTANT...
...METROPOLIS!
WHEN SUDDENLY...
GRAB!
YOINK!
WWSSH!

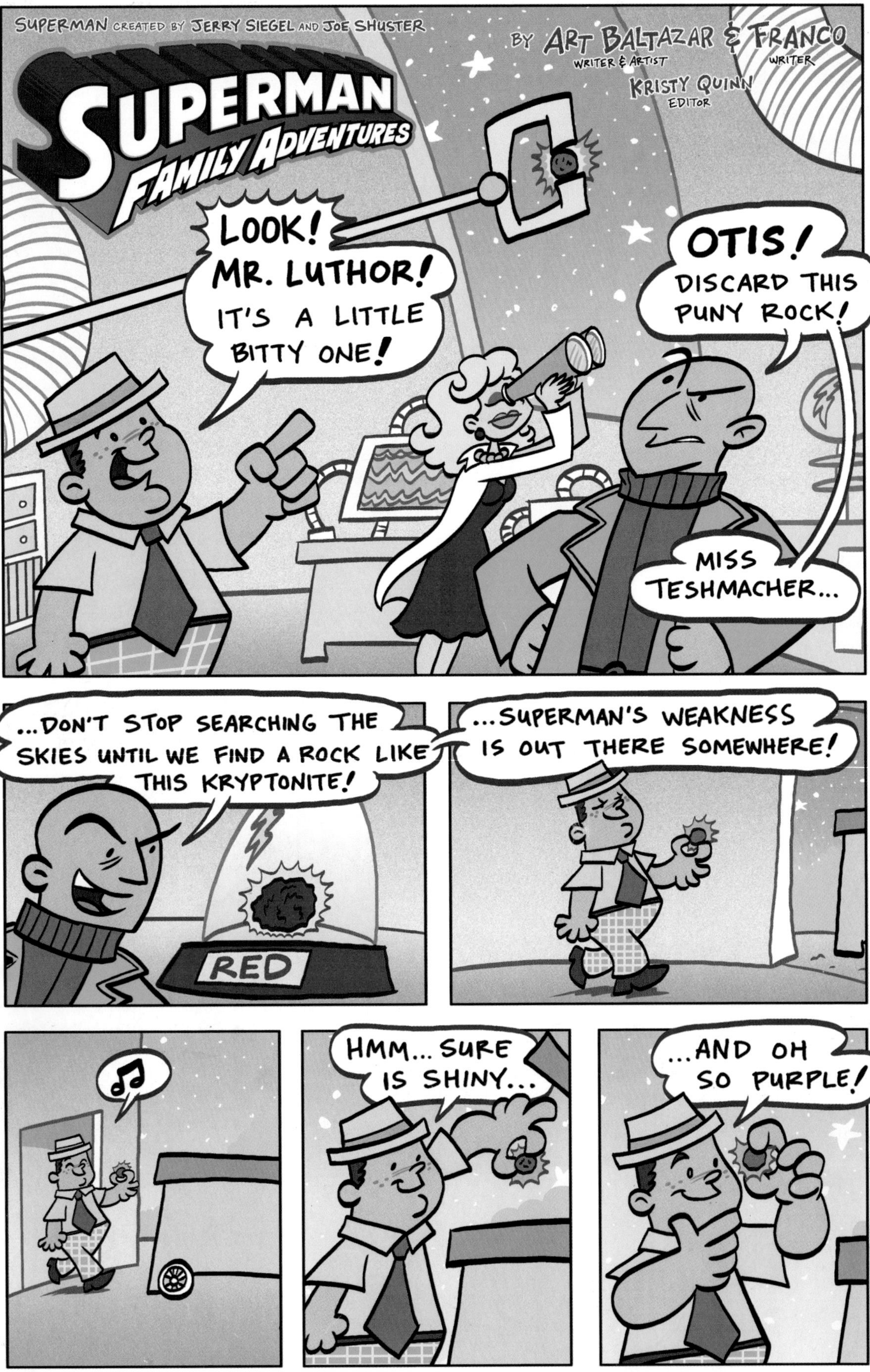
SUPERMAN CREATED BY JERRY SIEGEL AND JOE SHUSTER
SUPERMAN FAMILY ADVENTURES
BY ART BALTAZAR WRITER & ARTIST & FRANCO WRITER
KRISTY QUINN EDITOR
LOOK! MR. LUTHOR! IT'S A LITTLE BITTY ONE!
OTIS! DISCARD THIS PUNY ROCK!
MISS TESHMACHER...
...DON'T STOP SEARCHING THE SKIES UNTIL WE FIND A ROCK LIKE THIS KRYPTONITE!
...SUPERMAN'S WEAKNESS IS OUT THERE SOMEWHERE!
RED
HMM... SURE IS SHINY...
...AND OH SO PURPLE!

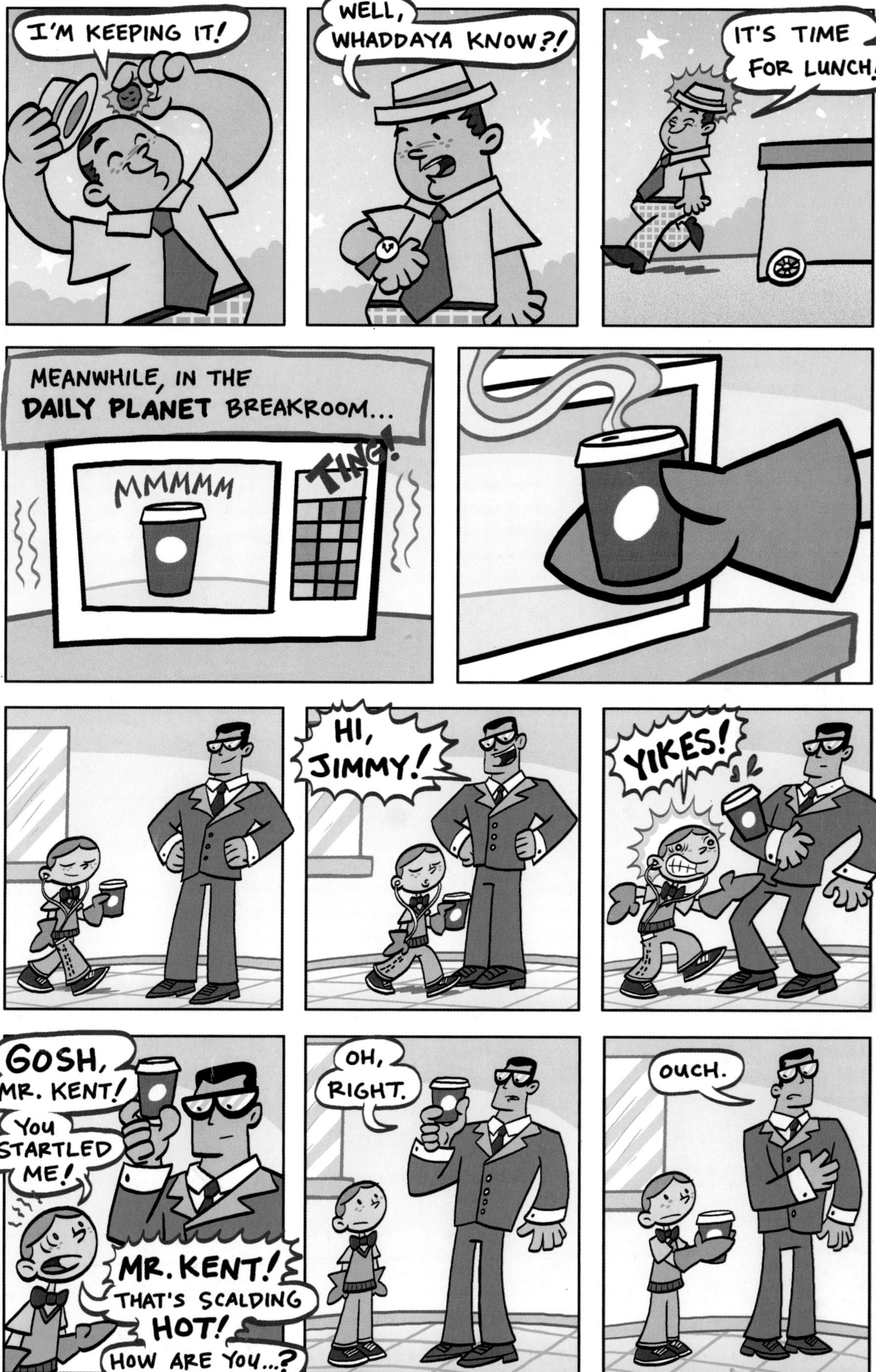

I'M KEEPING IT!
WELL, WHADDAYA KNOW?!
IT'S TIME FOR LUNCH!
MEANWHILE, IN THE DAILY PLANET BREAKROOM...
MMMMM
TING!
HI, JIMMY!
YIKES!
GOSH, MR. KENT!
YOU STARTLED ME!
MR. KENT! THAT'S SCALDING HOT!
HOW ARE YOU...?
OH, RIGHT.
OUCH.

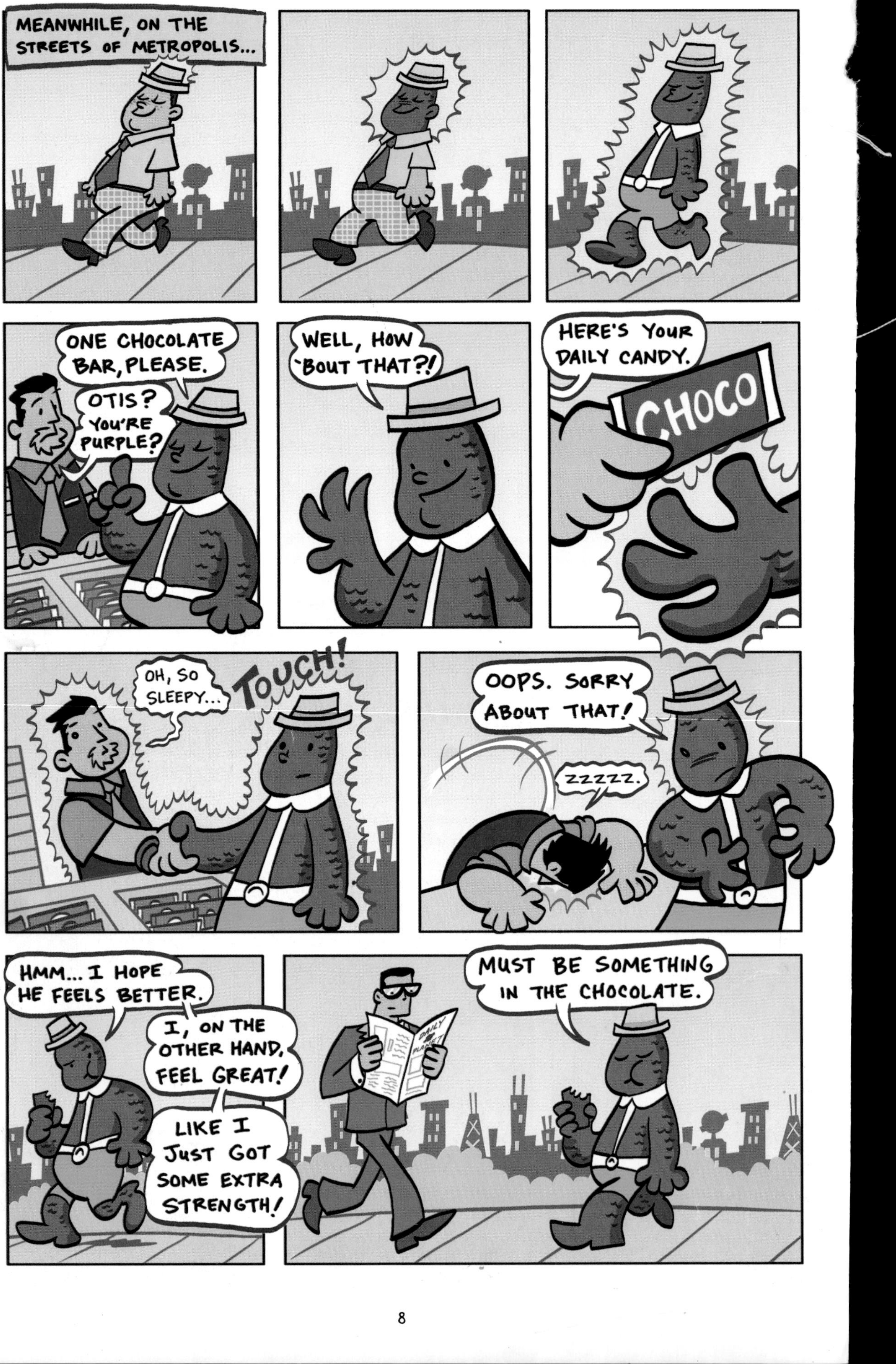
MEANWHILE, ON THE STREETS OF METROPOLIS...
ONE CHOCOLATE BAR, PLEASE.
OTIS? YOU'RE PURPLE?
WELL, HOW 'BOUT THAT?!
HERE'S YOUR DAILY CANDY.
CHOCO
OH, SO SLEEPY...
TOUCH!
OOPS. SORRY ABOUT THAT!
ZZZZZ.
HMM... I HOPE HE FEELS BETTER.
I, ON THE OTHER HAND, FEEL GREAT!
LIKE I JUST GOT SOME EXTRA STRENGTH!
MUST BE SOMETHING IN THE CHOCOLATE.

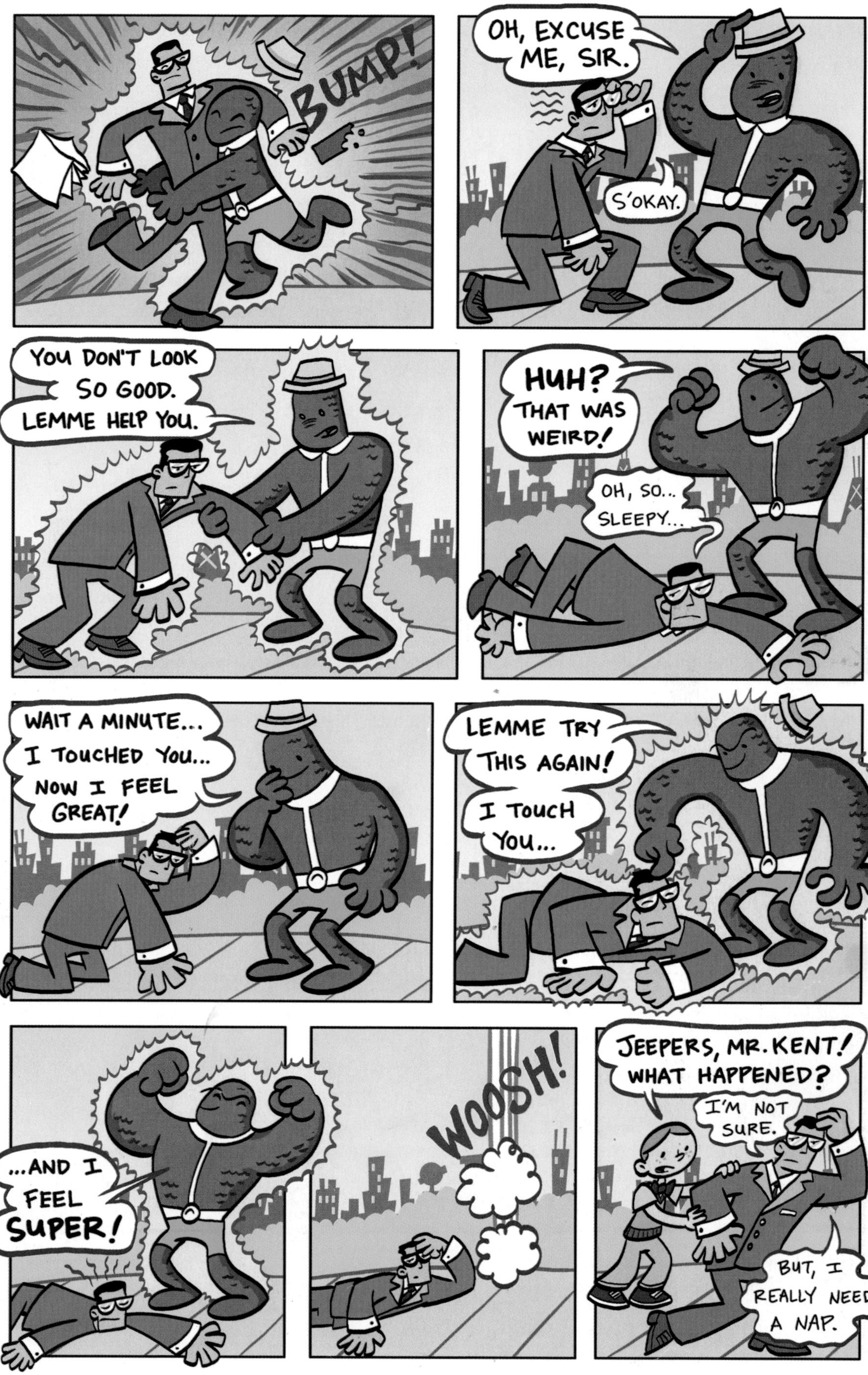
BUMP!
OH, EXCUSE ME, SIR.
S'OKAY.
YOU DON'T LOOK SO GOOD. LEMME HELP YOU.
HUH? THAT WAS WEIRD!
OH, SO... SLEEPY...
WAIT A MINUTE... I TOUCHED YOU... NOW I FEEL GREAT!
LEMME TRY THIS AGAIN!
I TOUCH YOU...
...AND I FEEL SUPER!
WOOSH!
JEEPERS, MR. KENT! WHAT HAPPENED?
I'M NOT SURE.
BUT, I REALLY NEED A NAP.

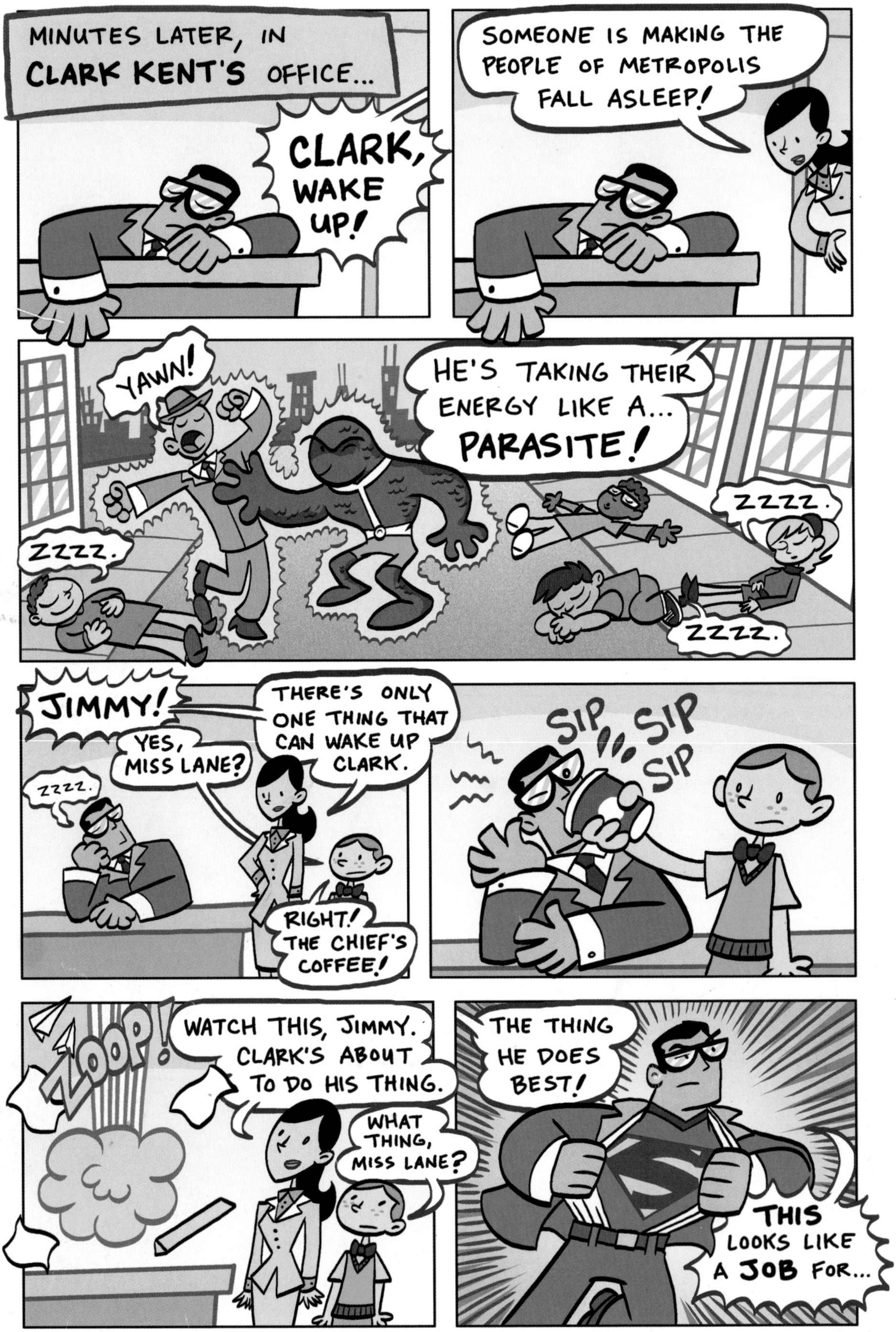
MINUTES LATER, IN CLARK KENT'S OFFICE...
CLARK, WAKE UP!
SOMEONE IS MAKING THE PEOPLE OF METROPOLIS FALL ASLEEP!
YAWN!
HE'S TAKING THEIR ENERGY LIKE A... PARASITE!
ZZZZ.
ZZZZ.
ZZZZ.
JIMMY!
THERE'S ONLY ONE THING THAT CAN WAKE UP CLARK.
YES, MISS LANE?
ZZZZ.
RIGHT! THE CHIEF'S COFFEE!
SIP SIP SIP
ZOOP!
WATCH THIS, JIMMY. CLARK'S ABOUT TO DO HIS THING.
WHAT THING, MISS LANE?
THE THING HE DOES BEST!
THIS LOOKS LIKE A JOB FOR...

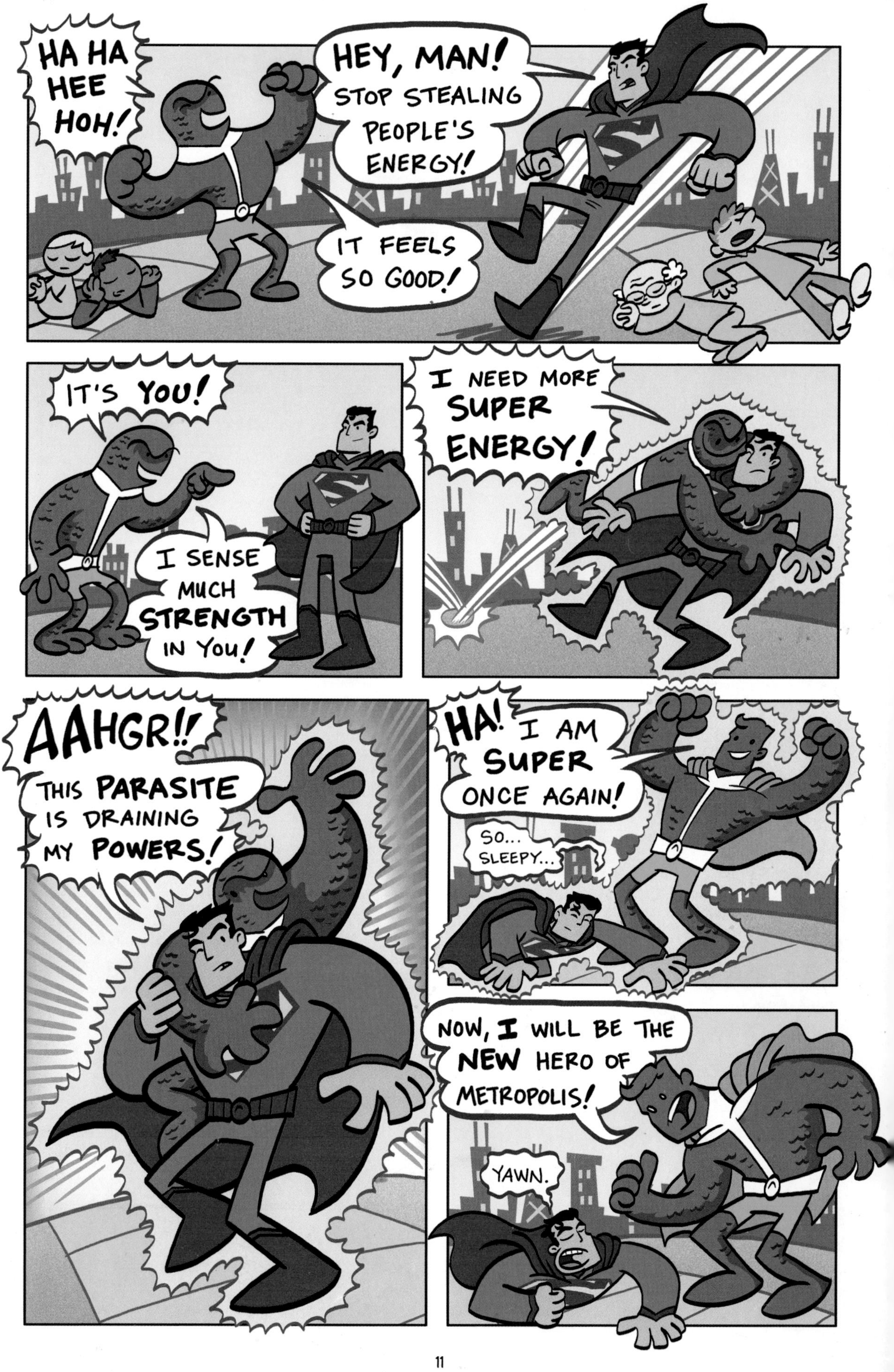
HA HA HEE HOH!
HEY, MAN! STOP STEALING PEOPLE'S ENERGY!
IT FEELS SO GOOD!
IT'S YOU!
I SENSE MUCH STRENGTH IN YOU!
I NEED MORE SUPER ENERGY!
AAHGR!! THIS PARASITE IS DRAINING MY POWERS!
HA! I AM SUPER ONCE AGAIN!
SO... SLEEPY...
NOW, I WILL BE THE NEW HERO OF METROPOLIS!
YAWN.

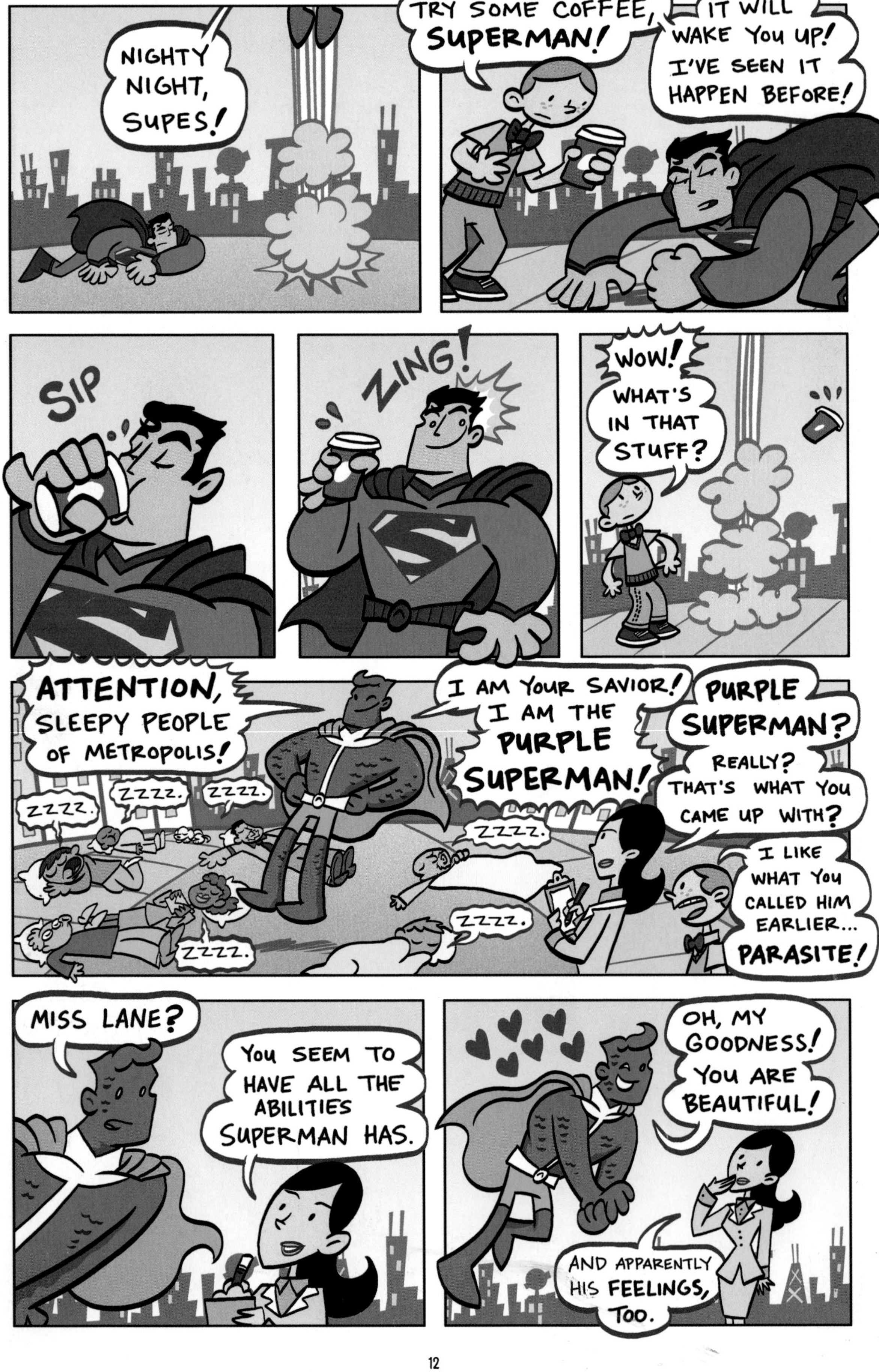

NIGHTY NIGHT, SUPES!
TRY SOME COFFEE, SUPERMAN!
IT WILL WAKE YOU UP! I'VE SEEN IT HAPPEN BEFORE!
SIP
ZING!
WOW!
WHAT'S IN THAT STUFF?
ATTENTION, SLEEPY PEOPLE OF METROPOLIS!
ZZZZ.
ZZZZ.
ZZZZ.
I AM YOUR SAVIOR! I AM THE PURPLE SUPERMAN!
ZZZZ.
ZZZZ.
ZZZZ.
PURPLE SUPERMAN?
REALLY? THAT'S WHAT YOU CAME UP WITH?
I LIKE WHAT YOU CALLED HIM EARLIER... PARASITE!
MISS LANE?
YOU SEEM TO HAVE ALL THE ABILITIES SUPERMAN HAS.
OH, MY GOODNESS! YOU ARE BEAUTIFUL!
AND APPARENTLY HIS FEELINGS, TOO.

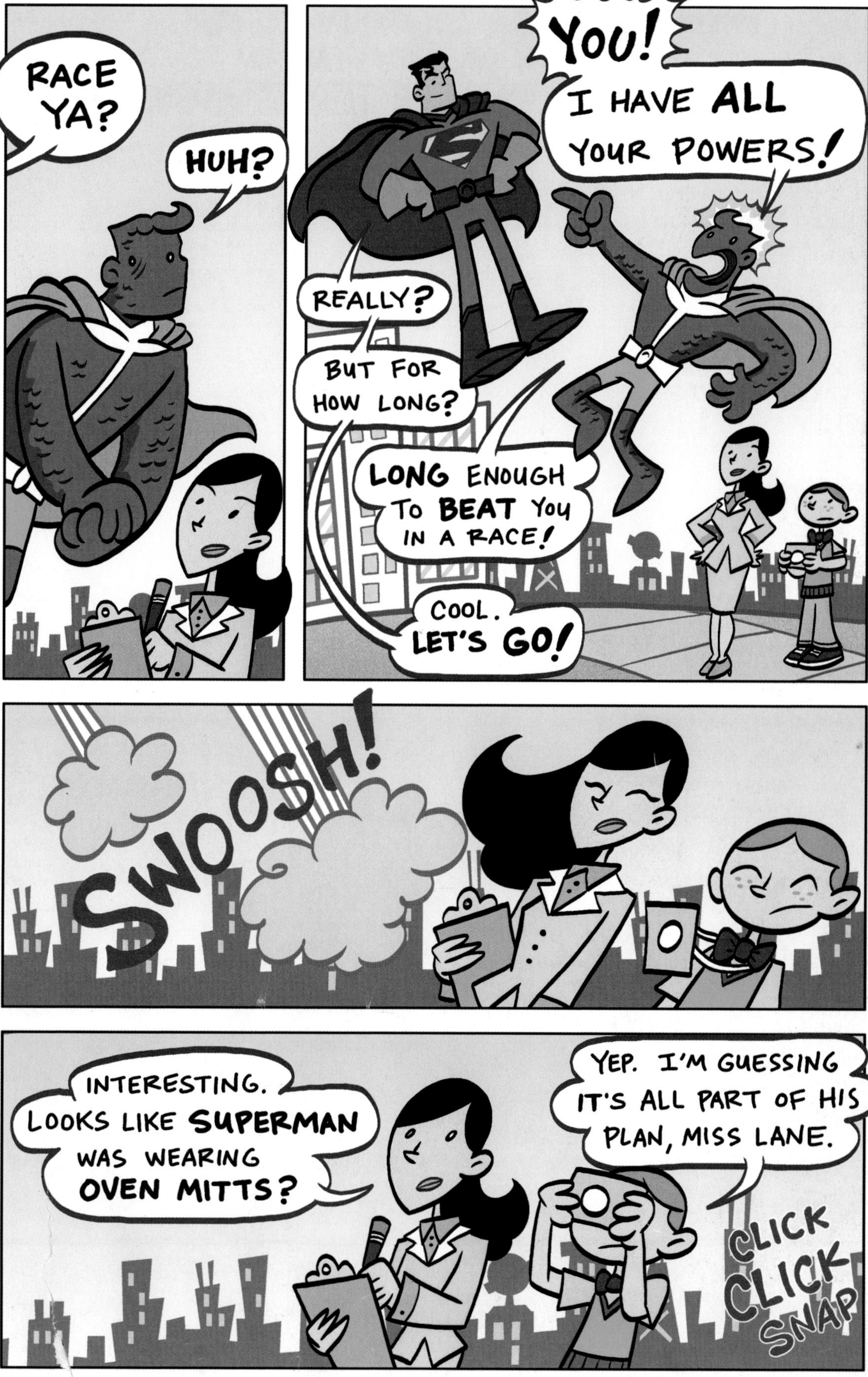
RACE YA?
HUH?
YOU!
I HAVE ALL YOUR POWERS!
REALLY?
BUT FOR HOW LONG?
LONG ENOUGH TO BEAT YOU IN A RACE!
COOL. LET'S GO!
SWOOSH!
INTERESTING. LOOKS LIKE SUPERMAN WAS WEARING OVEN MITTS?
YEP. I'M GUESSING IT'S ALL PART OF HIS PLAN, MISS LANE.
CLICK
CLICK
SNAP

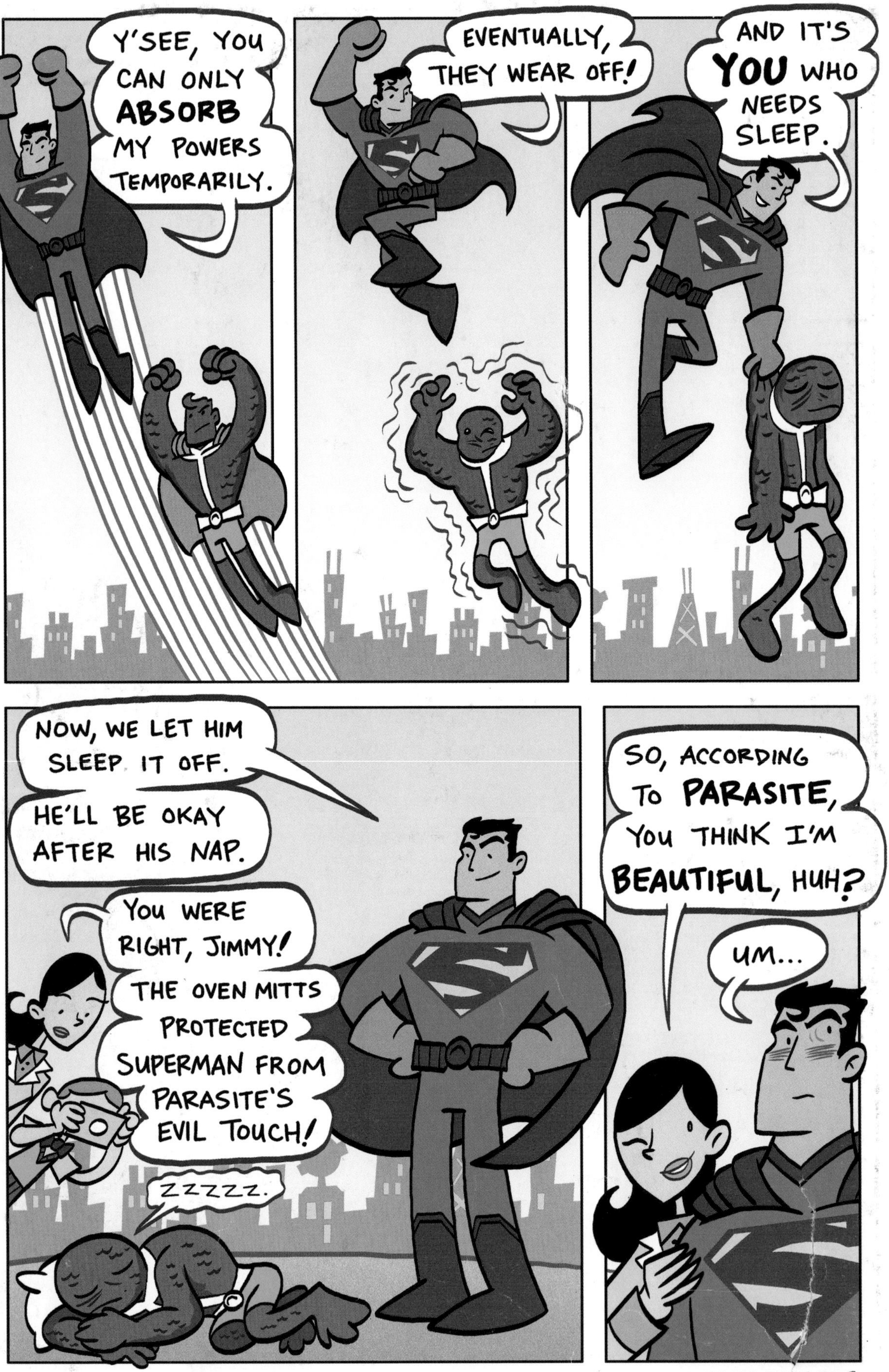
Y'SEE, YOU CAN ONLY **ABSORB** MY POWERS TEMPORARILY.
EVENTUALLY, THEY WEAR OFF!
AND IT'S **YOU** WHO NEEDS SLEEP.
NOW, WE LET HIM SLEEP IT OFF.
HE'LL BE OKAY AFTER HIS NAP.
YOU WERE RIGHT, JIMMY!
THE OVEN MITTS PROTECTED SUPERMAN FROM PARASITE'S EVIL TOUCH!
ZZZZZ.
SO, ACCORDING TO **PARASITE**, YOU THINK I'M **BEAUTIFUL**, HUH?
UM...

-THINK SHE GOTCHA, DUDE.

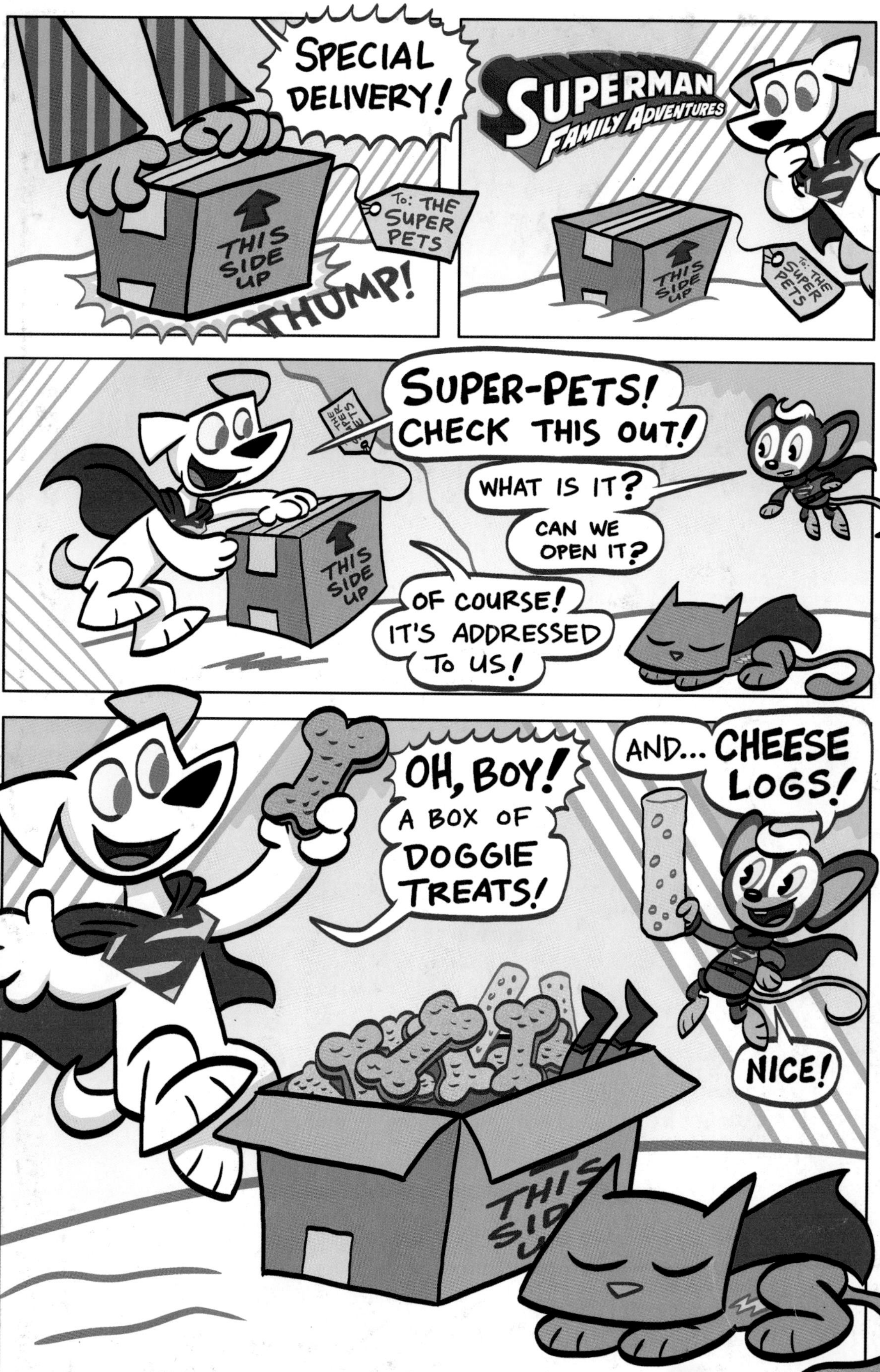
SPECIAL DELIVERY!
TO: THE SUPER PETS
THIS SIDE UP
THUMP!
SUPERMAN FAMILY ADVENTURES
TO: THE SUPER PETS
THIS SIDE UP
SUPER-PETS! CHECK THIS OUT!
WHAT IS IT?
CAN WE OPEN IT?
OF COURSE! IT'S ADDRESSED TO US!
THIS SIDE UP
OH, BOY! A BOX OF DOGGIE TREATS!
AND... CHEESE LOGS!
NICE!

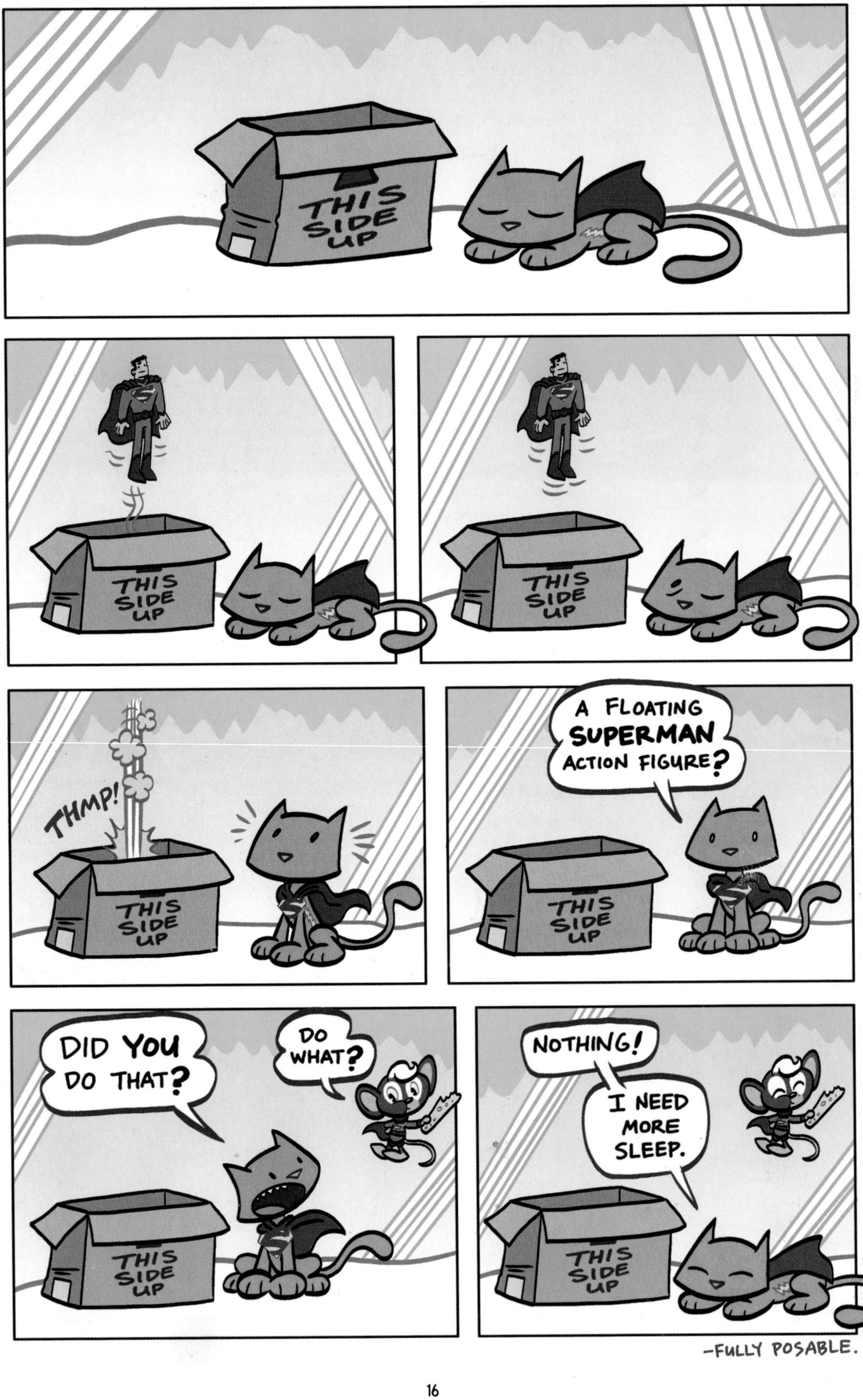
THIS SIDE UP
THMP!
A FLOATING SUPERMAN ACTION FIGURE?
DID YOU DO THAT?
DO WHAT?
NOTHING!
I NEED MORE SLEEP.
-FULLY POSABLE.

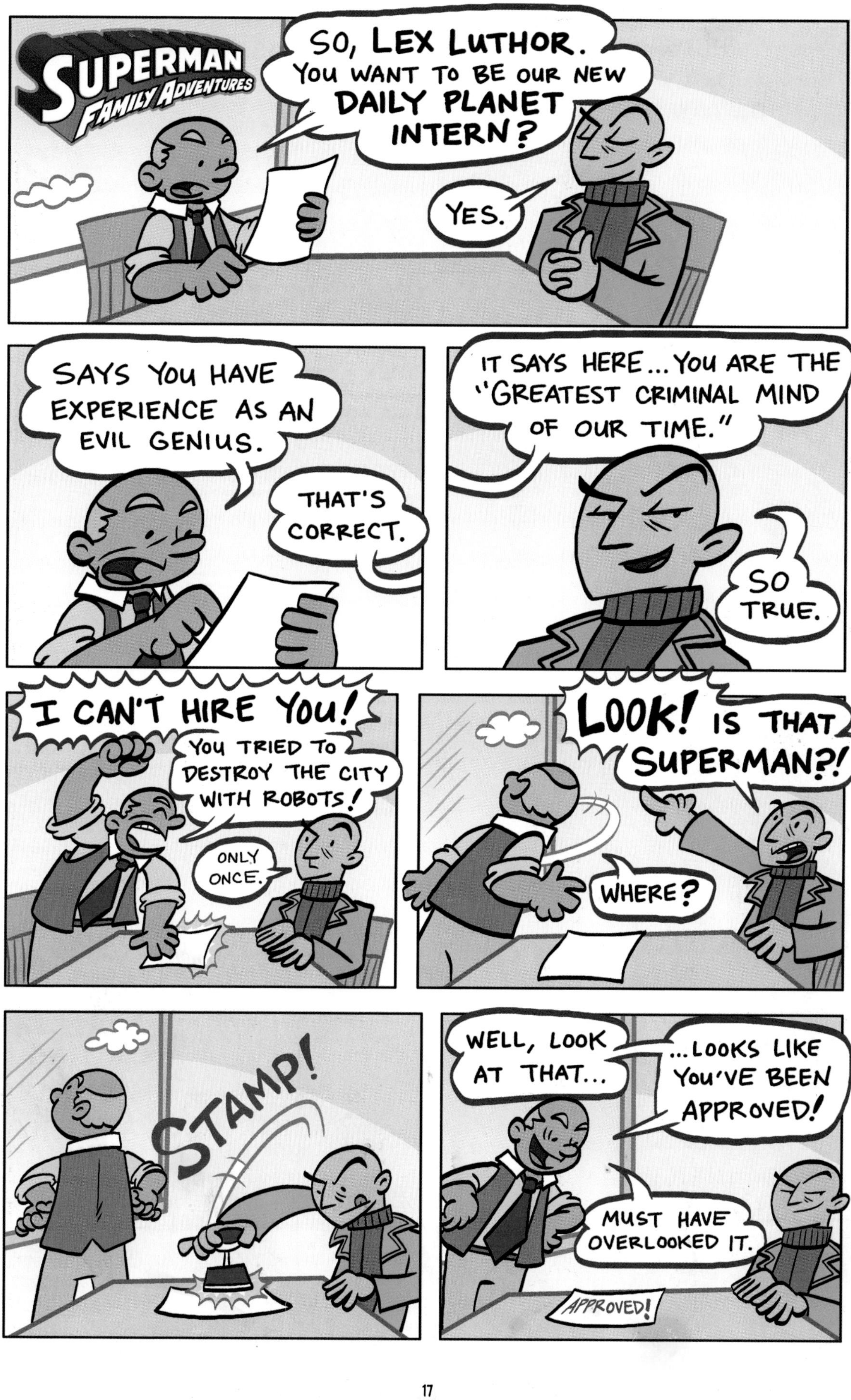
SUPERMAN FAMILY ADVENTURES
SO, LEX LUTHOR. YOU WANT TO BE OUR NEW DAILY PLANET INTERN?
YES.
SAYS YOU HAVE EXPERIENCE AS AN EVIL GENIUS.
THAT'S CORRECT.
IT SAYS HERE... YOU ARE THE "GREATEST CRIMINAL MIND OF OUR TIME."
SO TRUE.
I CAN'T HIRE YOU!
YOU TRIED TO DESTROY THE CITY WITH ROBOTS!
ONLY ONCE.
LOOK! IS THAT SUPERMAN?!
WHERE?
STAMP!
WELL, LOOK AT THAT...
...LOOKS LIKE YOU'VE BEEN APPROVED!
MUST HAVE OVERLOOKED IT.
APPROVED!

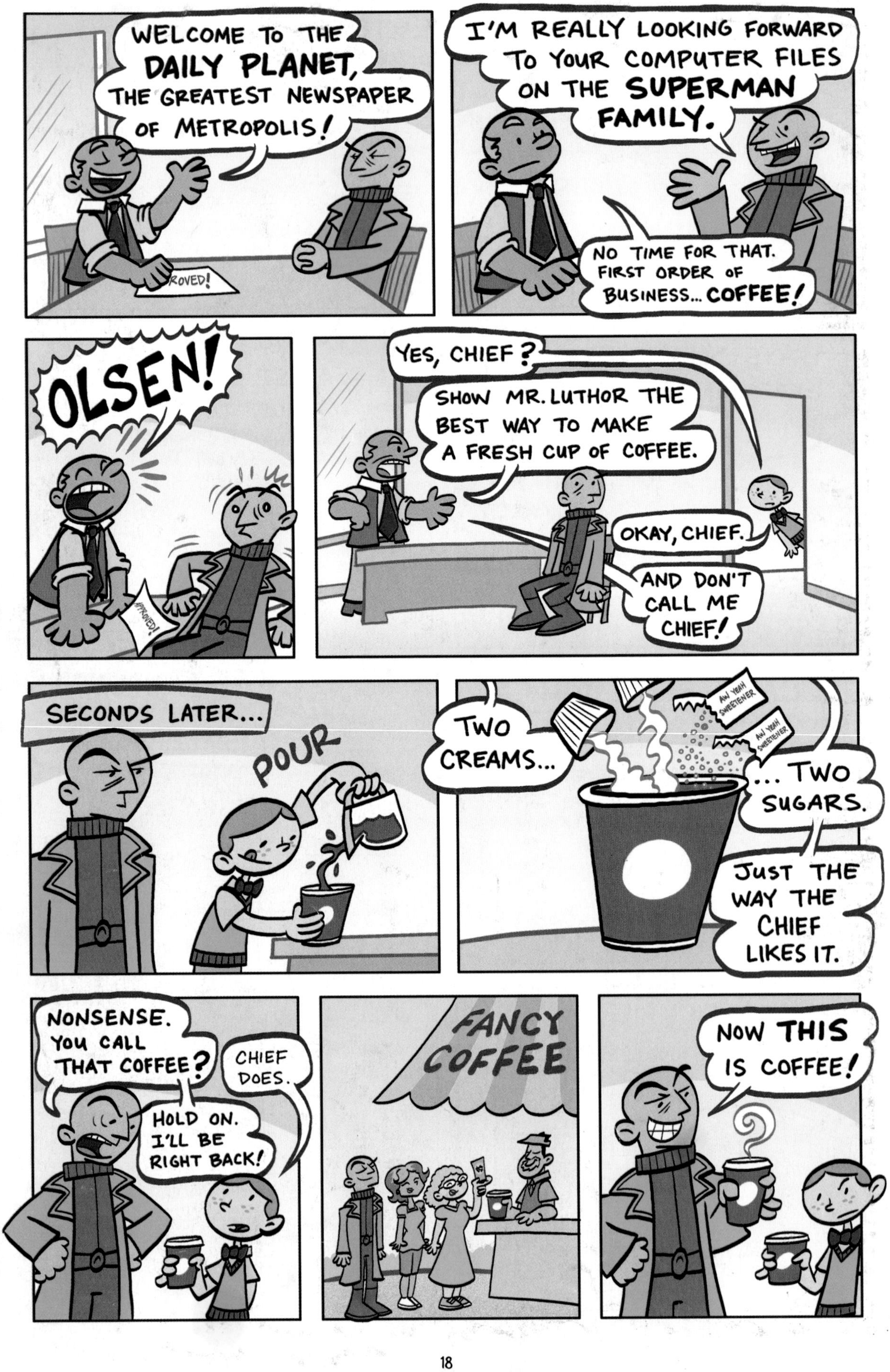
WELCOME TO THE DAILY PLANET, THE GREATEST NEWSPAPER OF METROPOLIS!
ROVED!
I'M REALLY LOOKING FORWARD TO YOUR COMPUTER FILES ON THE SUPERMAN FAMILY.
NO TIME FOR THAT. FIRST ORDER OF BUSINESS... COFFEE!
OLSEN!
APPROVED!
YES, CHIEF?
SHOW MR. LUTHOR THE BEST WAY TO MAKE A FRESH CUP OF COFFEE.
OKAY, CHIEF.
AND DON'T CALL ME CHIEF!
SECONDS LATER...
POUR
TWO CREAMS...
AW YEAH SWEETENER
AW YEAH SWEETENER
...TWO SUGARS.
JUST THE WAY THE CHIEF LIKES IT.
NONSENSE. YOU CALL THAT COFFEE?
CHIEF DOES.
HOLD ON. I'LL BE RIGHT BACK!
FANCY COFFEE
NOW THIS IS COFFEE!

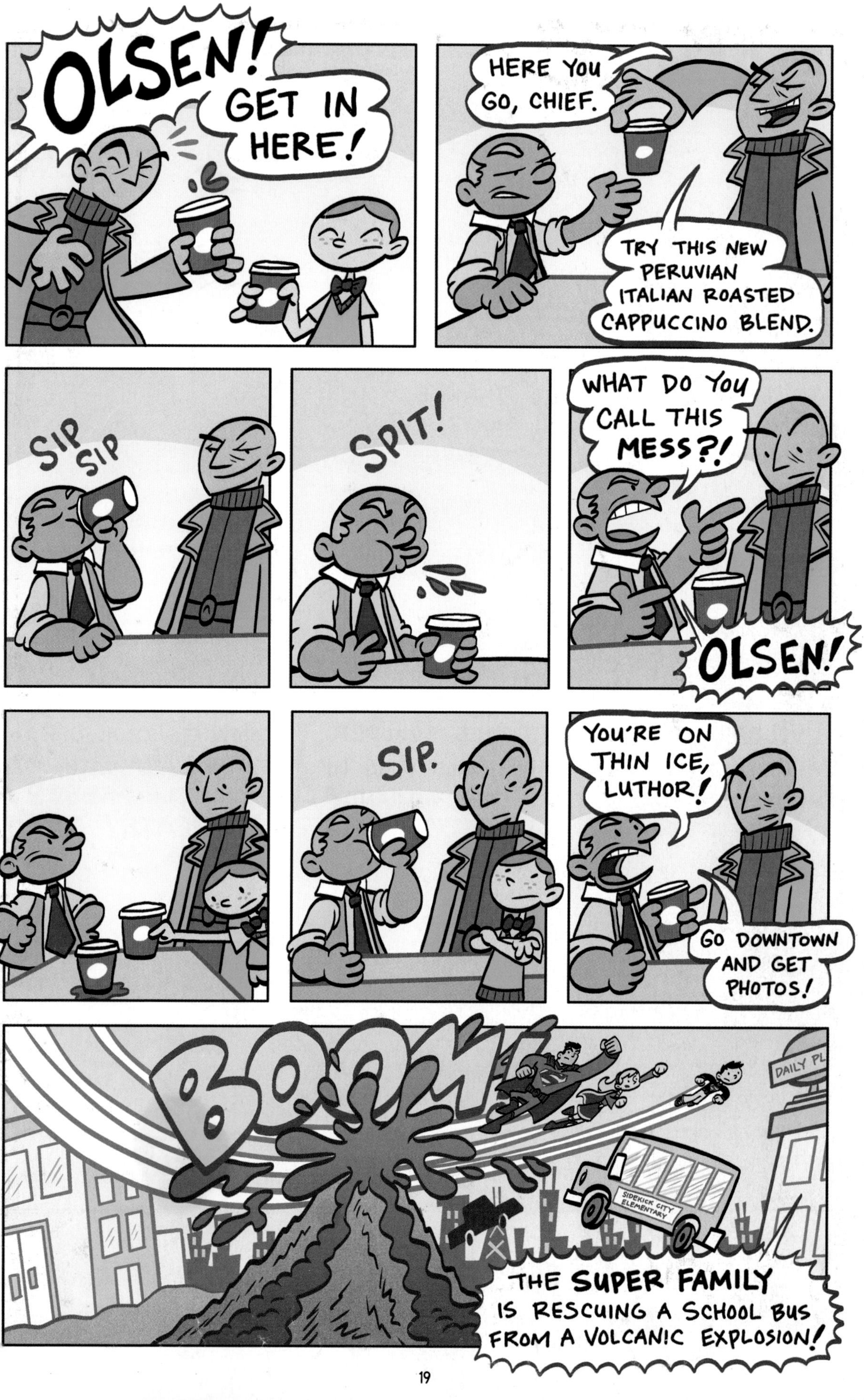
OLSEN!
GET IN HERE!
HERE YOU GO, CHIEF.
TRY THIS NEW PERUVIAN ITALIAN ROASTED CAPPUCCINO BLEND.
SIP SIP
SPIT!
WHAT DO YOU CALL THIS MESS?!
OLSEN!
SIP.
YOU'RE ON THIN ICE, LUTHOR!
GO DOWNTOWN AND GET PHOTOS!
BOOM!
DAILY PL
SIDEKICK CITY ELEMENTARY
THE SUPER FAMILY IS RESCUING A SCHOOL BUS FROM A VOLCANIC EXPLOSION!

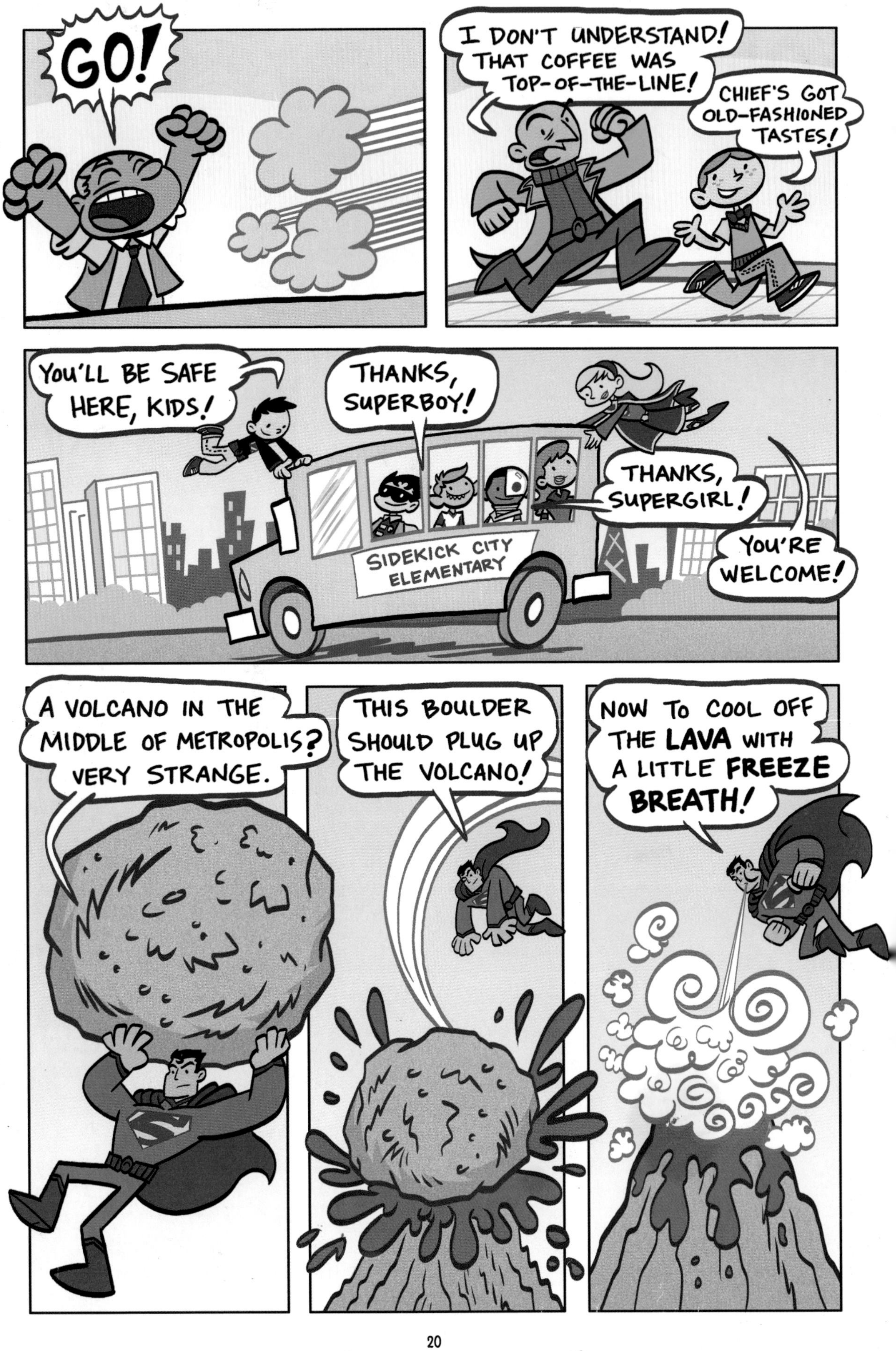
GO!
I DON'T UNDERSTAND! THAT COFFEE WAS TOP-OF-THE-LINE!
CHIEF'S GOT OLD-FASHIONED TASTES!
YOU'LL BE SAFE HERE, KIDS!
THANKS, SUPERBOY!
SIDEKICK CITY ELEMENTARY
THANKS, SUPERGIRL!
YOU'RE WELCOME!
A VOLCANO IN THE MIDDLE OF METROPOLIS? VERY STRANGE.
THIS BOULDER SHOULD PLUG UP THE VOLCANO!
NOW TO COOL OFF THE **LAVA** WITH A LITTLE **FREEZE BREATH**!

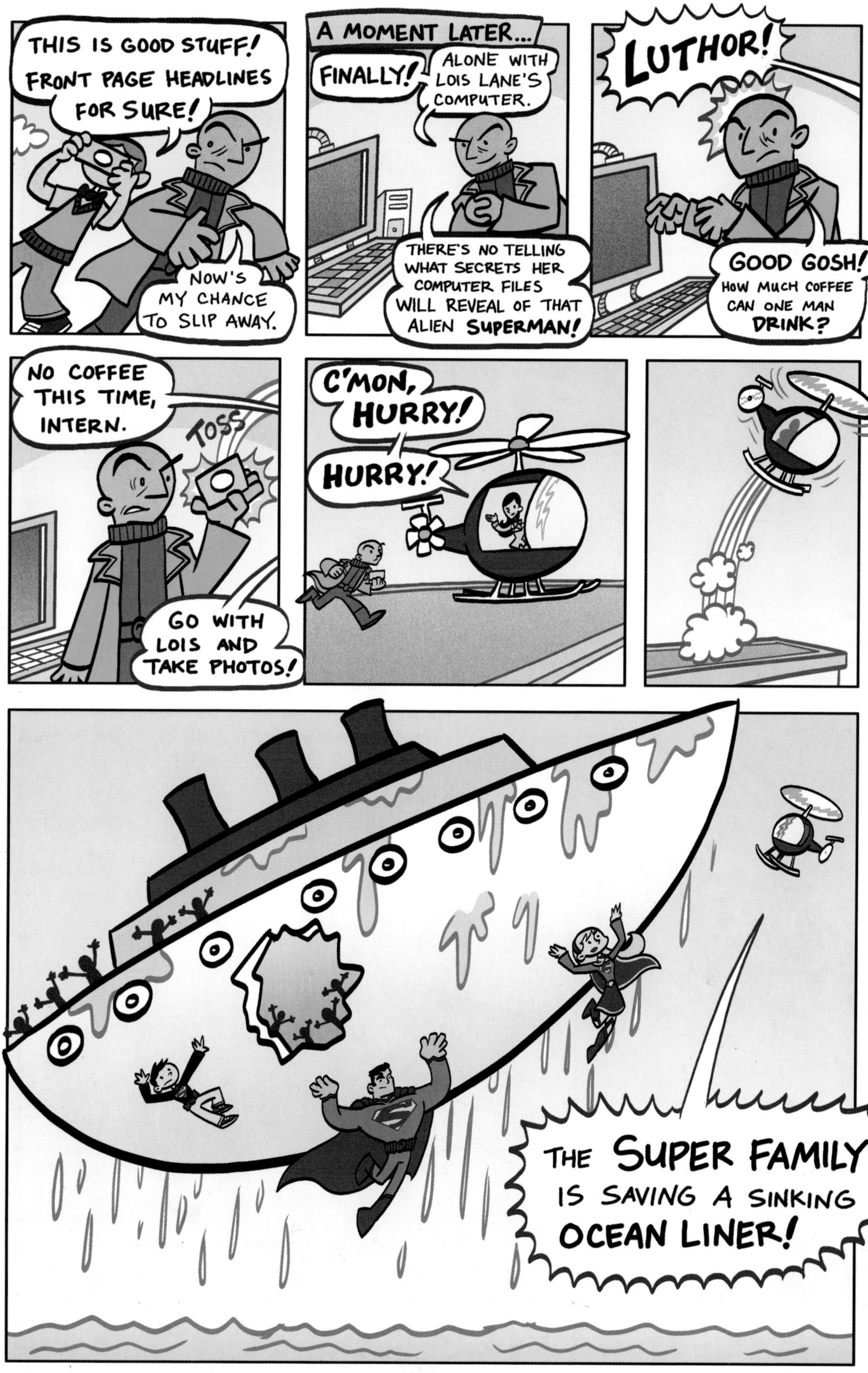
THIS IS GOOD STUFF! FRONT PAGE HEADLINES FOR SURE!
NOW'S MY CHANCE TO SLIP AWAY.
A MOMENT LATER...
FINALLY!
ALONE WITH LOIS LANE'S COMPUTER.
THERE'S NO TELLING WHAT SECRETS HER COMPUTER FILES WILL REVEAL OF THAT ALIEN SUPERMAN!
LUTHOR!
GOOD GOSH! HOW MUCH COFFEE CAN ONE MAN DRINK?
NO COFFEE THIS TIME, INTERN.
TOSS
GO WITH LOIS AND TAKE PHOTOS!
C'MON, HURRY!
HURRY!
THE SUPER FAMILY IS SAVING A SINKING OCEAN LINER!

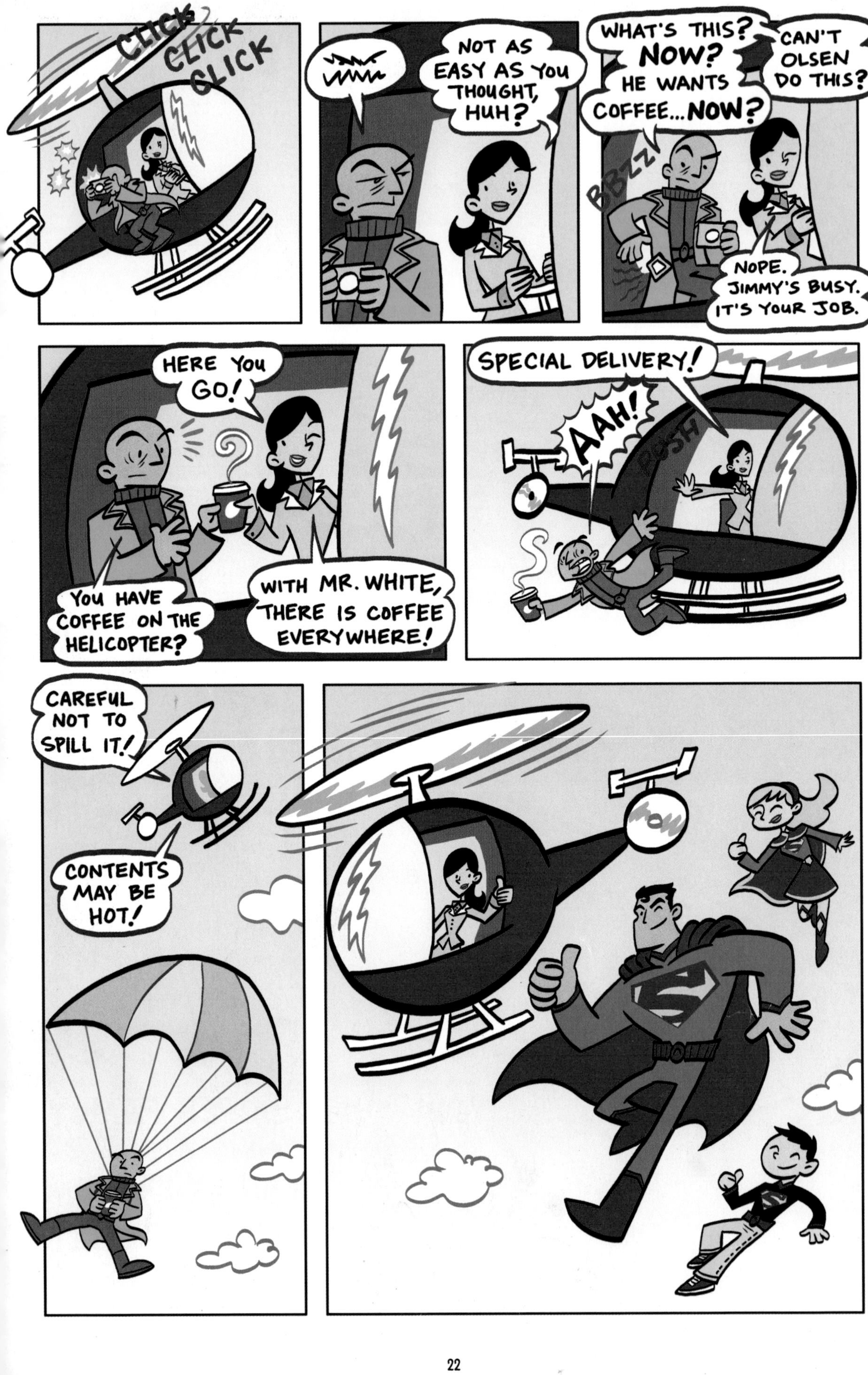
CLICK CLICK CLICK
NOT AS EASY AS YOU THOUGHT, HUH?
WHAT'S THIS? NOW? HE WANTS COFFEE...NOW?
CAN'T OLSEN DO THIS?
BBZZZ
NOPE. JIMMY'S BUSY. IT'S YOUR JOB.
HERE YOU GO!
YOU HAVE COFFEE ON THE HELICOPTER?
WITH MR. WHITE, THERE IS COFFEE EVERYWHERE!
SPECIAL DELIVERY!
AAH!
PUSH
CAREFUL NOT TO SPILL IT!
CONTENTS MAY BE HOT!

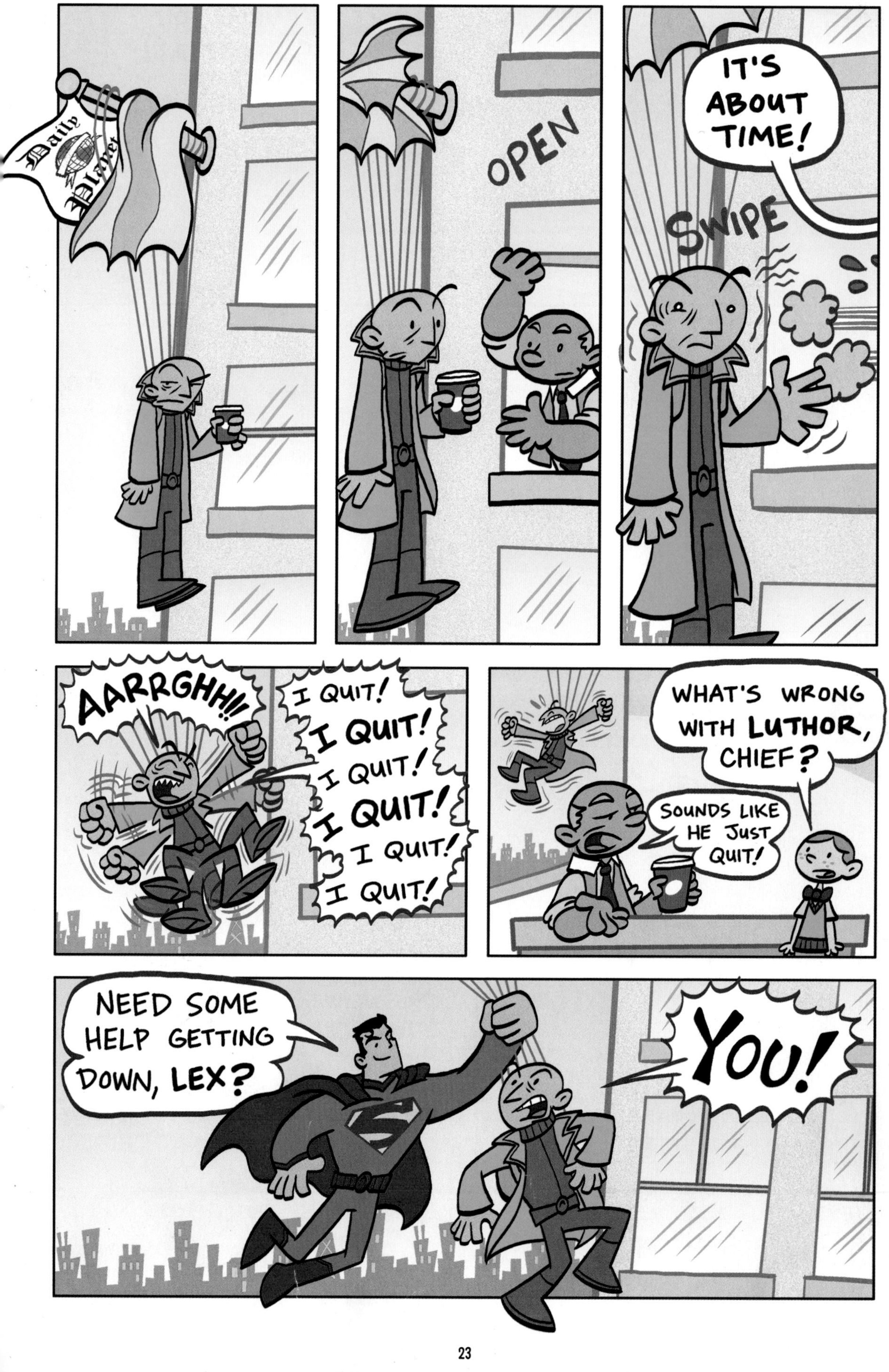
Daily Planet
OPEN
IT'S ABOUT TIME!
SWIPE
AARRGHH!!
I QUIT! I QUIT! I QUIT! I QUIT! I QUIT! I QUIT!
WHAT'S WRONG WITH LUTHOR, CHIEF?
SOUNDS LIKE HE JUST QUIT!
NEED SOME HELP GETTING DOWN, LEX?
YOU!

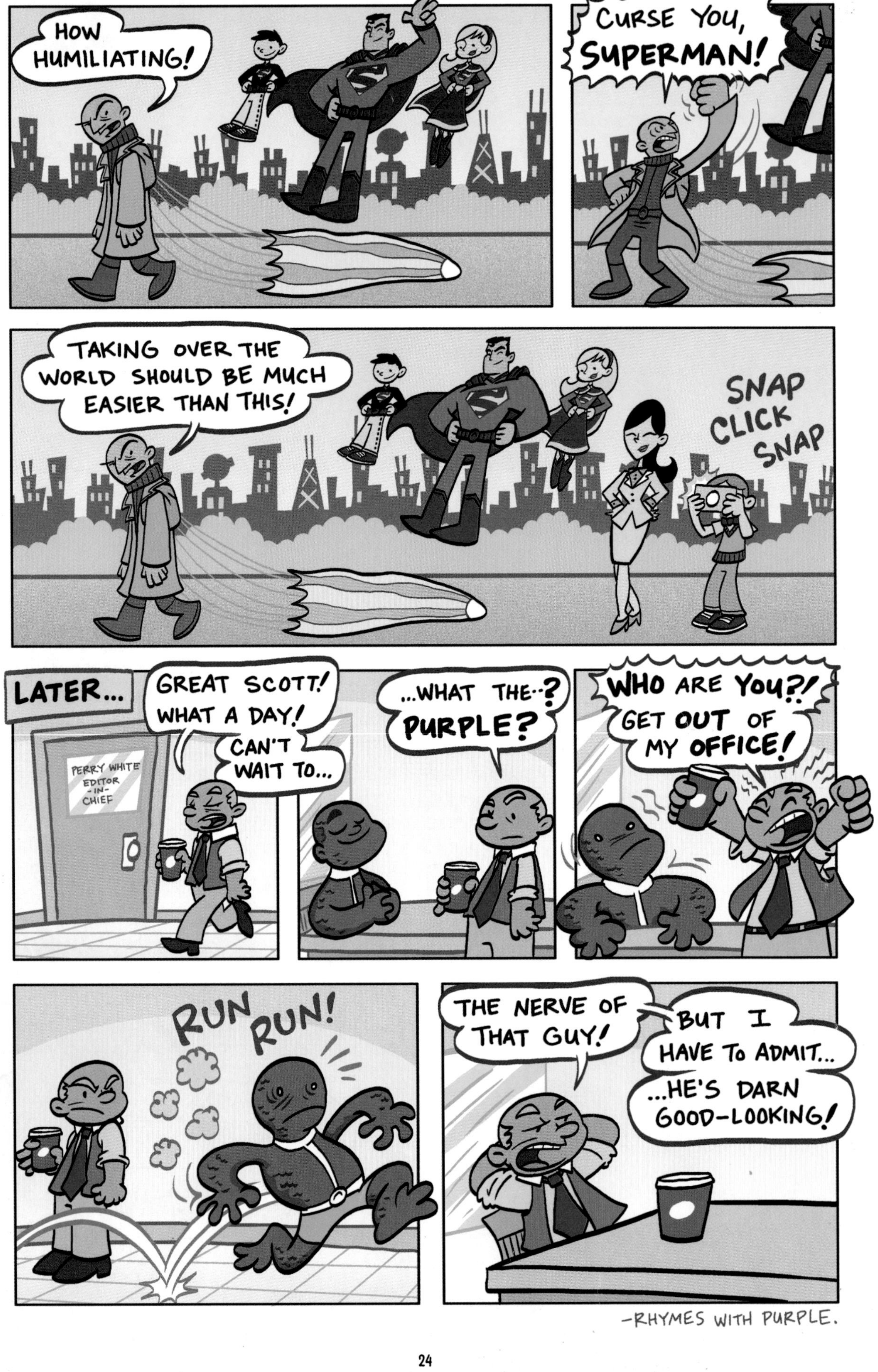
HOW HUMILIATING!
CURSE YOU, SUPERMAN!
TAKING OVER THE WORLD SHOULD BE MUCH EASIER THAN THIS!
SNAP CLICK SNAP
LATER...
GREAT SCOTT! WHAT A DAY!
CAN'T WAIT TO...
PERRY WHITE EDITOR -IN- CHIEF
...WHAT THE..? PURPLE?
WHO ARE YOU?! GET OUT OF MY OFFICE!
RUN RUN!
THE NERVE OF THAT GUY!
BUT I HAVE TO ADMIT...
...HE'S DARN GOOD-LOOKING!

-RHYMES WITH PURPLE.

SUPERMAN®
FAMILY ADVENTURES™

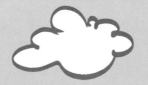

CREATORS

ART BALTAZAR IS A CARTOONIST MACHINE FROM THE HEART OF CHICAGO! HE DEFINES CARTOONS AND COMICS NOT ONLY AS AN ART STYLE, BUT AS A WAY OF LIFE. CURRENTLY, ART IS THE CREATIVE FORCE BEHIND THE NEW YORK TIMES BEST-SELLING, EISNER AWARD-WINNING, DC COMICS SERIES TINY TITANS, AND THE CO-WRITER FOR BILLY BATSON AND THE MAGIC OF SHAZAM! AND CO-CREATOR OF SUPERMAN FAMILY ADVENTURES. ART IS LIVING THE DREAM! HE DRAWS COMICS AND NEVER HAS TO LEAVE THE HOUSE. HE LIVES WITH HIS LOVELY WIFE, ROSE, BIG BOY SONNY, LITTLE BOY GORDON, AND LITTLE GIRL AUDREY. RIGHT ON!

ART BALTAZAR

FRANCO

FRANCO AURELIANI, BRONX, NEW YORK BORN WRITER AND ARTIST, HAS BEEN DRAWING COMICS SINCE HE COULD HOLD A CRAYON. CURRENTLY RESIDING IN UPSTATE NEW YORK WITH HIS WIFE, IVETTE, AND SON, NICOLAS, FRANCO SPENDS MOST OF HIS DAYS IN A BATCAVE-LIKE STUDIO WHERE HE PRODUCES DC'S TINY TITANS COMICS. IN 1995, FRANCO FOUNDED BLINDWOLF STUDIOS, AN INDEPENDENT ART STUDIO WHERE HE AND FELLOW CREATORS CAN CREATE CHILDREN'S COMICS. FRANCO IS THE CREATOR, ARTIST, AND WRITER OF WEIRDSVILLE, L'IL CREEPS, AND EAGLE ALL STAR, AS WELL AS THE CO-CREATOR AND WRITER OF PATRICK THE WOLF BOY. WHEN HE'S NOT WRITING AND DRAWING, FRANCO ALSO TEACHES HIGH SCHOOL ART.

GLOSSARY

ability (uh-BIL-i-tee)—a skill, or the power to do something

absorb (ab-ZORB)—to take in or suck or swallow up

cappuccino (kap-uh-CHEE-noh)—coffee made with frothy milk and often flavored with cinnamon

collision (kuh-LIZH-uhn)—the act or instance of crashing together forcefully, often at high speeds

discard (diss-KARD)—to get rid of as useless or unwanted

genius (JEEN-yuhss)—an unusually smart or talented person

humiliating (hyoo-MIL-ee-ate-ing)—causing a loss of pride or self-respect

intern (IN-turn)—someone who is learning a skill or a job by working with an expert in that field

meteorite (MEE-tee-ur-rite)—a remaining part of a meteor that falls to Earth before it has burned up

parasite (PA-ruh-site)— a living thing which lives in or on another living thing in parasitism

puny (PYOO-nee)—slight or lesser in power, size, or importance

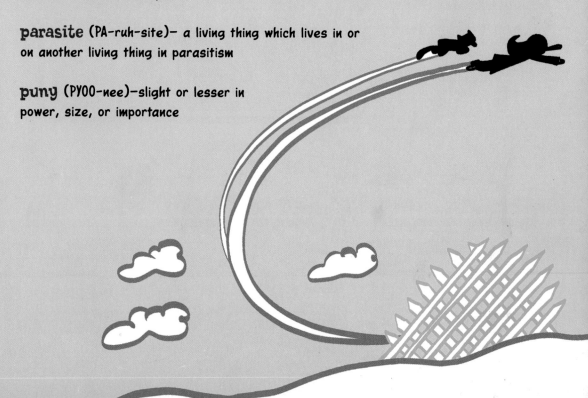

VISUAL QUESTIONS & PROMPTS

1. WHY DO YOU THINK THE PARASITE TAKES ON THE SHAPE OF SUPERMAN? USE EXAMPLES FROM THE STORY TO SUPPORT YOUR ANSWER.

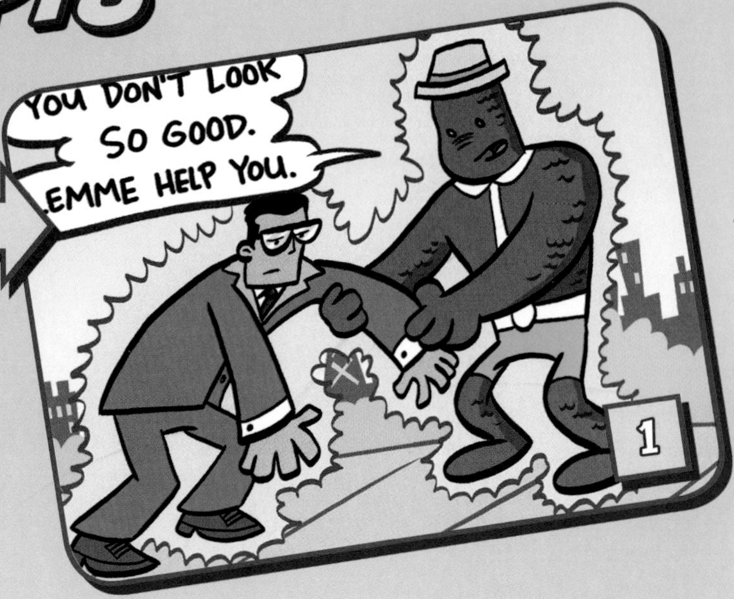
YOU DON'T LOOK SO GOOD. LEMME HELP YOU.
1

2. DO YOU THINK JIMMY OLSEN KNOWS THAT CLARK KENT IS REALLY SUPERMAN? EXPLAIN YOUR ANSWER.

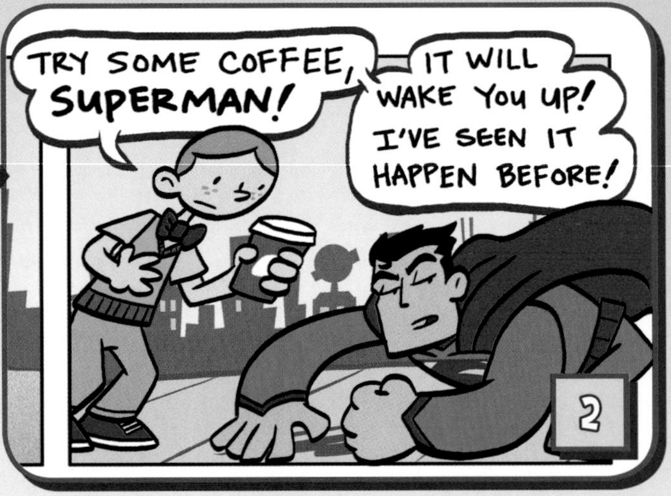
TRY SOME COFFEE, SUPERMAN!
IT WILL WAKE YOU UP! I'VE SEEN IT HAPPEN BEFORE!
2

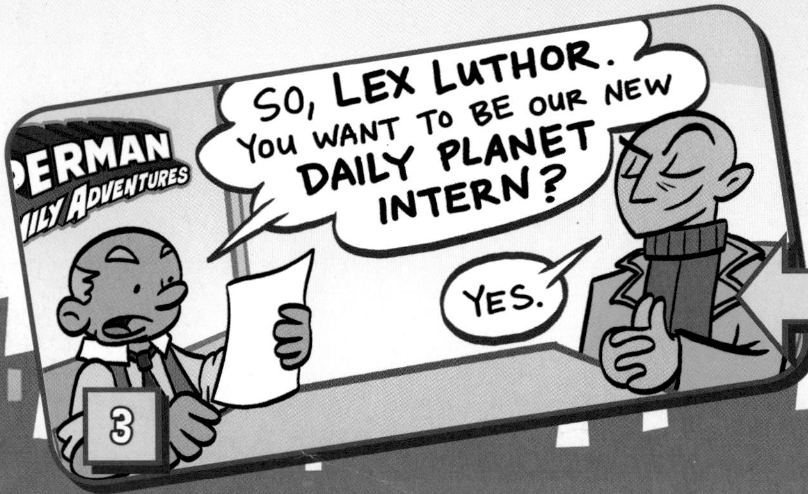
SO, LEX LUTHOR. YOU WANT TO BE OUR NEW DAILY PLANET INTERN?
YES.
3

3. WHY DO YOU THINK LEX LUTHOR WANTS A JOB AT THE *DAILY PLANET* NEWSPAPER?

4. THE WAY A CHARACTER'S EYES AND MOUTH LOOK, ALSO KNOWN AS THEIR FACIAL EXPRESSION, CAN TELL A LOT ABOUT THE EMOTIONS HE OR SHE IS FEELING. BELOW, HOW DO YOU THINK THE JIMMY OLSEN IS FEELING? USE THE ILLUSTRATION TO EXPLAIN YOUR ANSWER.

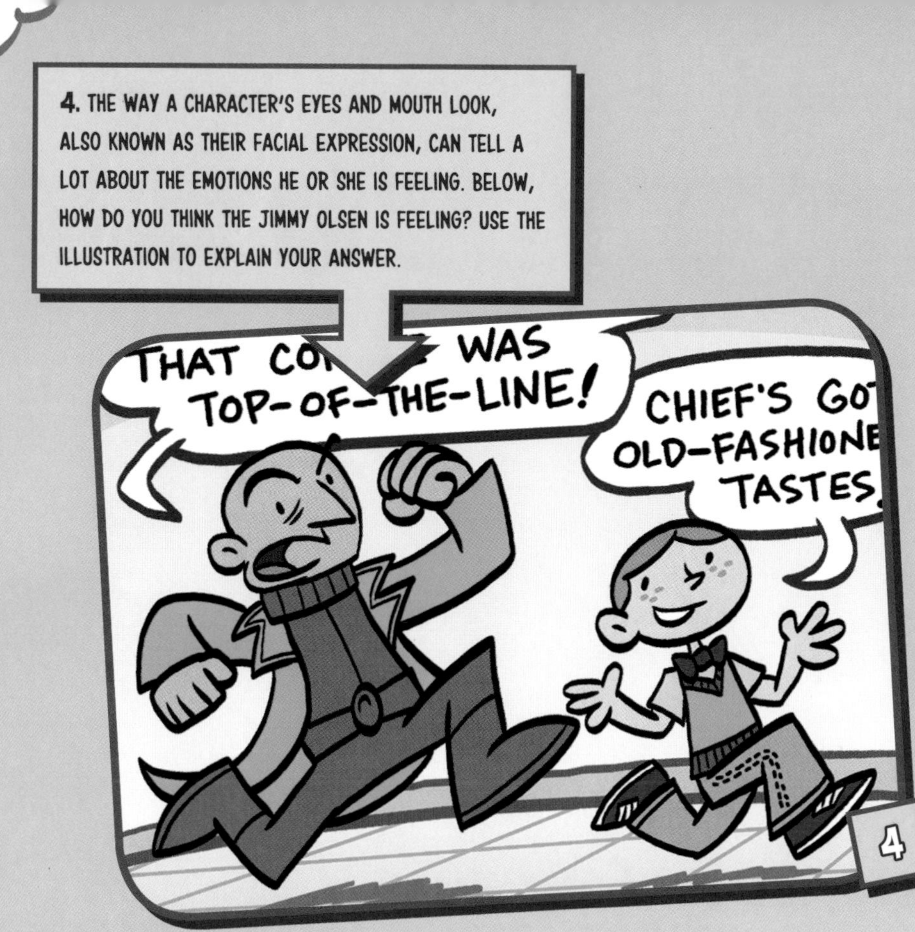
THAT CO WAS TOP-OF-THE-LINE!
CHIEF'S GOT OLD-FASHIONE TASTES.
4

5. SUPERMAN AND OTHER MEMBERS OF THE SUPER FAMILY HAVE MANY SUPERPOWERS, INCLUDING SUPER-STRENGTH, SUPER-SPEED, HEAT VISION, AND MORE. IF YOU COULD HAVE ANY SUPERPOWER, WHAT WOULD IT BE, AND WHY?

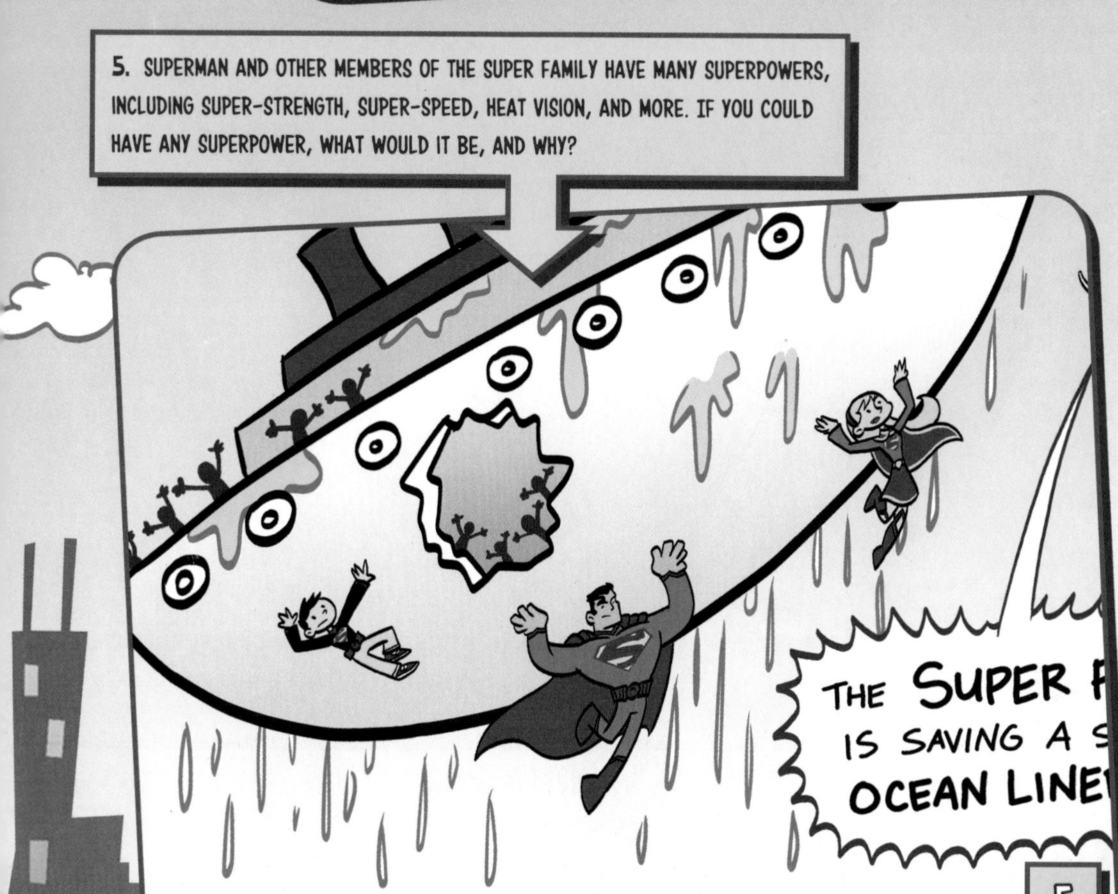
THE SUPER F
IS SAVING A S
OCEAN LINE
5

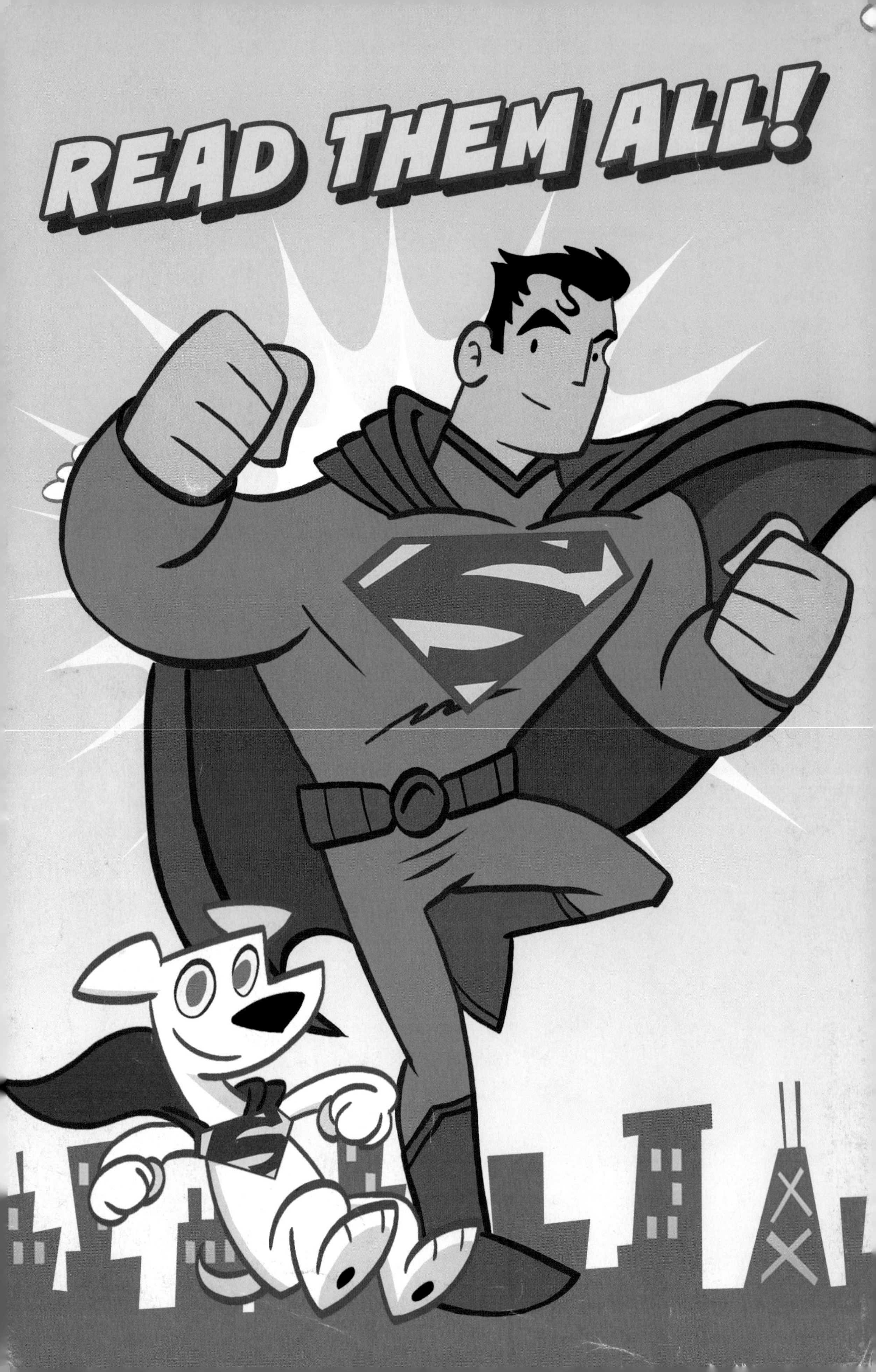
READ THEM ALL!

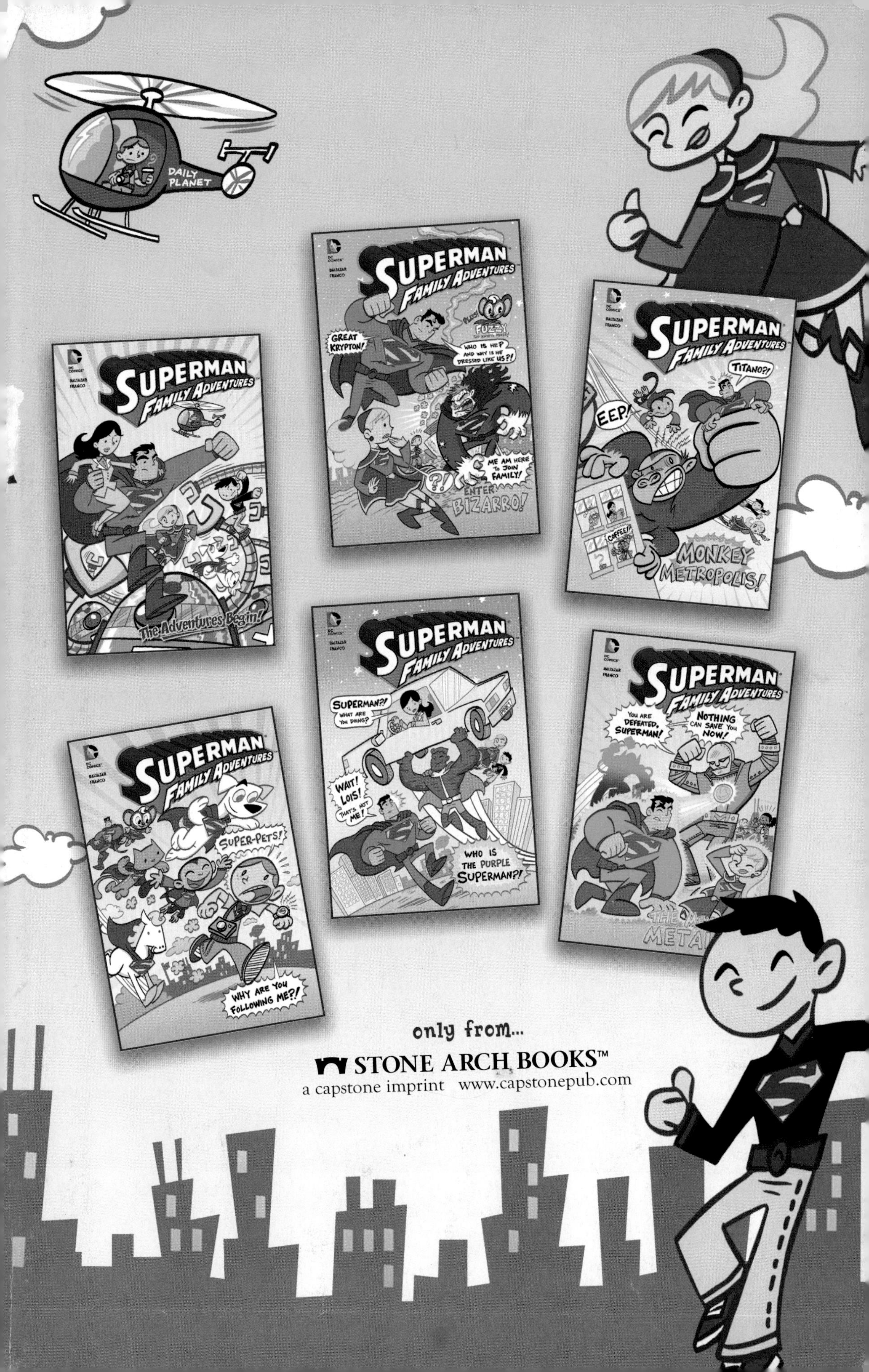
DAILY PLANET
SUPERMAN FAMILY ADVENTURES
BALTAZAR FRANCO
The Adventures Begin!
SUPERMAN FAMILY ADVENTURES
GREAT KRYPTON!
WHO IS HE? AND WHY IS HE DRESSED LIKE US?!
PLUS! FUZZY
ME AM HERE TO JOIN FAMILY!
?!
ENTER: BIZARRO!
SUPERMAN FAMILY ADVENTURES
TITANO?!
EEP!
COFFEE!
MONKEY METROPOLIS!
SUPERMAN FAMILY ADVENTURES
SUPER-PETS!
WHY ARE YOU FOLLOWING ME?!
SUPERMAN FAMILY ADVENTURES
SUPERMAN?! WHAT ARE YOU DOING?
WAIT! LOIS! THAT'S NOT ME!
WHO IS THE PURPLE SUPERMAN?!
SUPERMAN FAMILY ADVENTURES
YOU ARE DEFEATED, SUPERMAN!
NOTHING CAN SAVE YOU NOW!
only from...
STONE ARCH BOOKS™
a capstone imprint www.capstonepub.com

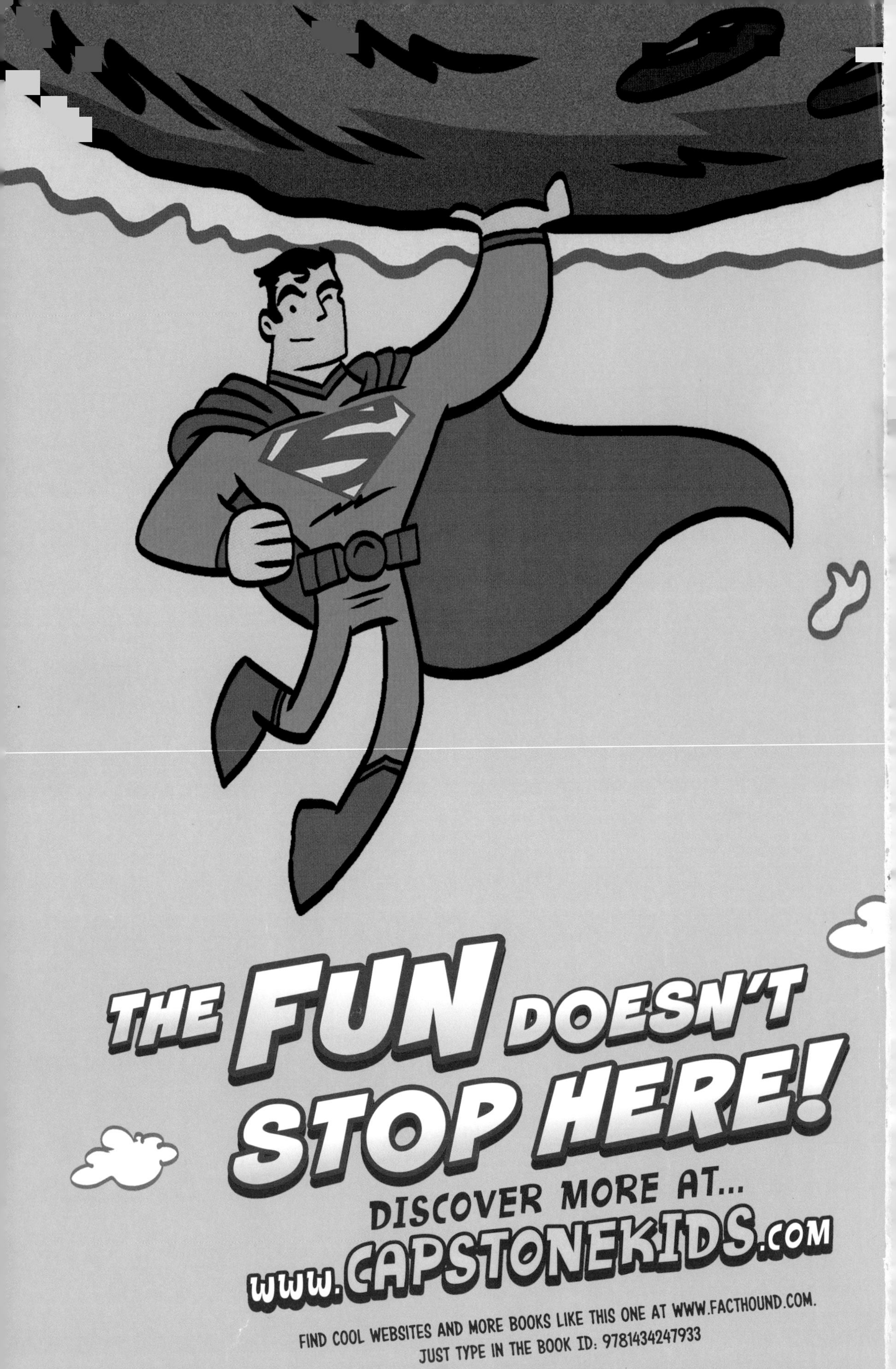